Sentinels at the Gates

A Telepathic Thriller

by

Joseph Patrick Rogers

Sentinels at the Gates

A Telepathic Thriller

The author’s website is **JoeRogers.homestead.com**

"If seeds in the black earth can turn into such beautiful roses, what might not the heart of man become in its long journey to the stars?"
G.K. Chesterton

"Every saint has a past and every sinner has a future."
Oscar Wilde

Prologue
Powers Mysterious

Rachel Kolbe, a young NSA agent, ran down the hallway of a top-secret National Security Agency building. Her green eyes shone with desperation.

At the end of this hallway, three persons were seated at an oval conference table: Nathanial Parker, the psy-ops unit director, met with Julie Constant, a psy-ops analyst/instructor, and Tim Carney, the security chief.

"Are you sure that we've been infiltrated?" Tim asked.

"We're about 80 percent sure," Julie replied.

"The terrorists are always one step ahead of us. After they disrupted the peace conference, we located their base of operations, but they were gone by the time our team got there," Nathaniel said.

"Maybe the team was too slow getting there," Tim suggested.

"Or maybe the terrorists were tipped off that we were coming," Julie said.

At that moment, Rachel stumbled into the conference room and crashed into the table, knocking over coffee cups and soda cans.

Everyone jumped to their feet.

"What the heck?" Tim exclaimed.

Julie rushed up to Rachel.

"Rachel!"

Rachel stood upright. "The infiltrator! The traitor! I know who!"

"What's wrong?" Julie asked.

"My brain! They're in my brain!" Rachel screamed.

"Who is it? What is the traitor's name?" Tim asked.

Rachel screamed again. "I can't … I can't say it!"

She screamed a third time. "Can't remember it."

Rachel collapsed onto the table, convulsed, then lay

still.

"Call an ambulance!" Nathaniel declared.

Tim bent down to examine Rachel. "It's too late! She's dead!"

"God bless her!" Julie said.

"Amen," Nathaniel said.

Julie cradled Rachel's body.

Tears filled Julie's eyes. "This wonderful young woman … this precious life … what evil has entered the world … and who can stop it?"

Chapter 1
Andrew's Tale
Powers Manifest

I drove my old, beat-up blue Chevy down a street in a middle-class neighborhood. I had recently turned 32 years old and just started growing a beard.

My father, Edward Preston, was about to turn 70 and somehow managed to look distinguished despite the fact that he was sitting on a curb.

Furniture, suitcases, paintings, clothing, and other possessions were piled up on the sidewalk and lawn near him.

I got out of my car.

"Father, what's going on?"

"I'm moving," he replied.

"Moving? Just out of the blue? Without telling me?"

"I'm spontaneous like that."

"Yeah, right," I said. "What's the story here?"

"I'm being evicted. I'm behind on rent."

"Oh."

"Since your mother passed . . . without her pension, it's been a challenge to keep up with the bills."

"Why didn't you ask me for help?"

"Well, I don't know . . . I guess that I should have, but . . ."

"But I got laid off two months ago, and I'm still looking for work," I said.

I sat on the curb next to him.

"Your Uncle Al is going to bring his truck to pick up me and my stuff," my father said. "I can stay with him for a while."

"This is ridiculous! You shouldn't be in this position. Neither of us should be! I have fantastic powers! I might be the only person in the world with these powers!"

"It's wise to keep quiet about those powers . . . those gifts."

"Why? Where has that gotten us? I've kept quiet about them for years. I haven't made a dime from these powers."

"You weren't given those gifts in order to make money."

"Then what good are they? Why do I have them?" I asked.

"We need to be patient. As time unfolds, the purpose

of the powers will become clear."

The landlord, a frowning middle-aged man, approached us.

"You can't leave all this stuff out here much longer. When will the truck be here?"

"Soon . . . a few minutes probably," my father said.

I stood up and looked at the landlord.

"Can I speak with you?" I asked him.

"I suppose so."

"Andrew . . . " my father said.

"I'll be nice."

The landlord and I walked a short distance away.

"My father is a good man and shouldn't be treated this way. It's embarrassing for him to be sitting out here with all his possessions."

"Then he needs to pay his rent."

"He can't give you money that he doesn't have," I said.

"Can you pay?"

"How much does he owe?"

"$2200"

"I can give you $700 today and a few hundred more next week."

"I need the entire $2200 today."

"You're a wealthy man. You don't need the entire $2200 today."

"I do," the landlord insisted.

I made a decision. I stared at the landlord, then mindjacked him.

"How much cash do you have in your wallet?" Andrew asked.

"About $3000."

"Why so much?"

"I collected rent from other tenants today."

"Give me $2500."

"Okay."

The landlord handed me the money. I placed the money in my wallet. Both of us placed our wallets back in our pockets.

I released the landlord from the mindjack.

"So you say that you need the entire amount today?" I asked.

The landlord's glazed stare and glassy eyes cleared as he emerged from the trance.

"Huh? What? Oh, yeah. I got distracted by something. Yes."

I took out my wallet and counted out $2200 in cash, which I handed to the landlord.

"I need a receipt," I said.

"Okay."

The landlord wrote a receipt and handed it to me.

"Thanks."

I walked back to Edward.

"Okay, Father, I paid your rent. You can move your furniture and stuff back inside."

"How did you . . . ?"

"I recently had some good luck at the casino."

"Hmmm. Well, thank you, Andrew."

We gathered up my father's belongings.

Two hours later, I drove along an urban street. Seeing a homeless man huddled on the sidewalk, I stopped the car, got out, and handed $300 to the man.

"I hope that this money helps, my friend."

"Thank you so much! God bless you!"

"You too!"

I got back in his car and drove away, feeling good about the events of that day.

Chapter 2
Mindjacker

Two weeks later, I was driving a new, expensive car.

After parking, I casually walked across the parking lot. A bored-looking security guard stood at the entrance to the bank.

"How's it going?" I asked with a friendly smile as I passed the guard.

"Pretty good," he replied.

I went into the lobby of the bank, pausing for a few moments to enjoy the new art display in the gallery. The display featured some attractive landscape paintings of seashores, mountains, waterfalls, and other scenic vistas.

I sat down in a comfortable chair next to a cactus. My carefully-selected seat was only a few feet away from the office of the bank's president. Glancing into his office, I saw that he was seated at his desk. I leaned a large briefcase against the glass wall near his office door.

Jake Gleason was a middle-aged man with a

pleasant smile and thick glasses. I focused upon his face as I relaxed and allowed my thoughts to drift toward him. My eyes closed, and I began to hear his thoughts. Within a few seconds, my consciousness and his shared the same body.

I opened the eyes of his body. His eyes had closed for several seconds as I took control. We shared his body, but I was completely in control. I took control so subtly and so gently that Jake didn't even realize that there was a problem.

I projected the idea to Jake that the customer sitting in the chair outside Jake's office was waiting for his money. Jake got up and walked out of his office, picking up my briefcase before heading across the lobby.

As the bank president, he could have opened the vault and given me access to over a million dollars. However, opening the vault would have attracted some attention, and I didn't want to take any chances. I wasn't greedy. The money in the workroom would be sufficient.

Moving swiftly and efficiently, I had Jake fill the briefcase with large denomination bills. When the briefcase was almost filled to capacity, I was startled by a bank clerk who entered the workroom.

Cindy Roberts looked surprised to see Jake standing at a table with a cash-filled briefcase in front of him. Fortunately, Jake did not realize that he was doing anything wrong, so no sign of tension appeared on his face.

"A customer is closing his account and wants his money in cash," Jake explained to Cindy.

"Doesn't he want us to transfer the funds electronically to his new bank?" she asked.

"I don't think that there is a new bank," Jake said with a grin. "I suppose that he's going to bury the money in his backyard or place it in a mattress."

As Cindy laughed, Jake snapped the briefcase shut and left the workroom. He walked across the lobby and placed the briefcase next to the chair where I was seated.

Jake went back into his office, sat in his chair, placed his head on the desk, and fell asleep. I withdrew my consciousness from him. When he awakened, he probably wouldn't remember going into the workroom and taking the cash.

I opened my eyes and picked up my briefcase as I stood. In a relaxed, unhurried manner, I strolled out of the bank.

"Have a good afternoon," I told the security guard.

"Thanks, you too," he waved goodbye to me.

I certainly will have a good afternoon, I thought with a laugh as I got in my car and drove away.

My favorite target was high-end jewelry stores. Jewelry stores had less security than banks. I only needed to mindjack the sales clerk or the owner, then walk out with a bag of diamond rings, gold necklaces, and a lot of cash.

I now lived a life of luxury and had purchased an expensive condominium in the best part of town.

I even contribute some money to charity. I suppose that I could be considered a modern-day Robin Hood. I steal from the rich and give to the poor. Well, truthfully, I give mainly to myself, but I was poor until very recently.

If I'm a Robin Hood, I'm a Robin Hood with weird, telepathic powers. These powers first manifested themselves when I was an adolescent. There were a couple of bullies who used to harass me. By sheer willpower, I tried to make them leave me alone. Gradually, through some mysterious means, I gained some control of their behavior. Then I gained complete control of them.

I never harmed them, though. I once had them fight each other, but stopped the fight before either of them was injured. After a short while, I lost interest in the bullies and sought no revenge against them. In fact, I was rather grateful to them because they had helped me discover my great powers.

In college, I occasionally read the minds of my professors in order to get the answers to tests and improve my grades.

Every year my telepathic abilities became stronger, perhaps from practice or perhaps from some natural evolution. In either case, I became stronger and sought new challenges.

Perhaps because I was starting to find robbing banks so easy and boring, I became careless. I went back to the same bank a second time. That was a foolish mistake. Four weeks after robbing Jake Gleason's bank, I returned with the intention of robbing it again.

I greeted the same security guard, went inside, and took the same seat outside of the bank president's office. Once again I placed my empty briefcase against the glass wall near his door.

Two of Jake's colleagues were meeting with him in the office. I could have mindjacked him in the middle of the meeting, but I decided to wait for his colleagues to leave. In order not to look suspicious sitting there, I took out my phone and checked for messages.

I was glad that Jake had not been arrested or fired as a result of my previous theft. The loss of so much money had surely been noticed, but apparently no one had been able to connect Jake Gleason to the theft.

After twenty minutes passed, I became impatient. I was not going to wait any longer. Just as I prepared to mindjack him, three men in suits approached me.

"Excuse me, sir," said one of the men.

"Yes?" I looked up at him.

"Could we speak with you for a minute in the conference room?" he asked, but it was a command, not a request.

"Why?" As I stood, I studied the faces of the three men. I was sure that they were either police or bank security officers.

"I'll explain when we are in the conference room," said the man who seemed to be in charge.

"Very well."

The other two men walked behind me as I followed the man in charge into the empty conference room, which was adjacent to the president's office.

"My name is David Hummel," the man said. "I'm with the FBI. These gentlemen are also FBI agents."

"What is this about, Mr. Hummel?" I asked.

"Could I see some identification?"

I took out my wallet, removed my driver's license, and handed it to David Hummel. He looked at it for a few seconds, then passed it along to the other two agents. One of those agents walked across the conference room and began typing on his phone, probably checking to see if I had a criminal record and if there were any warrants for my arrest.

"Is there a problem, Mr. Hummel?"

"Why are you visiting the bank today, Mr. Preston?"

"I want to open a money market account here," I said.

"Why did you bring an empty briefcase?" another FBI agent asked, opening my briefcase that he had picked up from next to the bank president's office.

"I often carry a briefcase. Since I was going to be opening a money market account, I figured that there would be some paperwork about the account to take home with me."

"There wouldn't be enough papers for you to need a briefcase," the second agent said.

I shrugged. "Maybe not. In any case, carrying a briefcase isn't a crime. Why am I being detained?"

"Four weeks ago, a large sum of money was stolen from this bank," Hummel said. "Upon reviewing the recordings of the security cameras, we saw you seated in the same chair in which you were seated today."

"I'm sure that there were many other persons in the bank that day," I said defensively.

"Yes, but you can be seen clearly in the video recordings by security cameras in other banks and jewelry stores that were robbed recently," Hummel said.

I was becoming very nervous. This was the first time that I had ever been confronted about what I had done. I had brought this trouble upon myself by being careless.

"Well?" David Hummel looked at me intently.

I briefly considered mindjacking him, then apologizing to myself and telling myself that I could leave. However, the two other FBI agents would surely notice such an abrupt change in behavior.

It might be possible to mindjack simultaneously Hummel and one of the other agents. I had never previously mindjacked two persons at once, but I thought that I was now strong enough to do so. However, this was not the right occasion to try such a thing. And there were three agents in the room with me. I knew that there was no way that I could mindjack all three of them simultaneously! Perhaps someday I would be capable of doing such a thing.

"Did you rob those banks and jewelry stores?" Hummel asked.

"Of course not."

"Then how do you account for your presence in each place on the day of the robbery?"

"I have no idea. I suppose that I have a knack for being in the wrong place at the wrong time."

"You're lying," the second agent said harshly. "Did you hypnotize persons in the banks and jewelry stores? Is that how you got them to give you money and jewelry?"

"That's ridiculous," I said. "Hypnosis? You've got to be kidding me."

"That's one theory that has been presented,"

Hummel said. "I'm personally skeptical about hypnosis, but I suppose that it's possible."

"It seems very unlikely," I said. "I have no idea how the thefts were carried out, though. Can I leave?"

"Not yet. Mr. Preston, you seem to me to be a good man. I am wondering whether you somehow got involved with something that got out of control. Why don't you just tell me what you know about these thefts?"

"I'm sorry. I can't help you."

"Okay."

Hummel and the second agent walked over to the third agent who had been using his phone to do online research about me. The three agents conferred for about two minutes, then approached me.

Hummel gave me back my driver's license and my briefcase. He also handed me his business card.

"You are free to go for now, Mr. Preston. However, we're going to need to talk to you again soon, so stay in town for the next few days. You can call me anytime if you would like to discuss this case. I promise that I will try to help you out if you tell me everything that you know about the thefts."

"Thank you, Agent Hummel." I placed his card into

my shirt pocket. "I have no information about the thefts, but I appreciate your courteousness."

I shook hands with Hummel, then walked out of the conference room. Hummel was an intelligent guy. He knew that I was somehow involved in the thefts, but he couldn't figure out how the thefts had been carried out.

As I went past the bank president's office, I saw Jake Gleason and several bank employees staring at me. They had been aware that the FBI was in the conference room questioning a suspect. I self-consciously continued my trek across the lobby aware that a number of persons were watching me.

As I stepped outside, I came face-to-face with the security guard with whom I had spoken previously.

"Hey, what happened in there?" he asked. "Why were those FBI agents talking to you?"

"Oh, it was just a misunderstanding," I said with feigned casualness. "Everything seems to be okay now."

"That's good."

After saying goodbye to him, I got in my car and drove away without delay. I wanted to get home as soon as possible. My condo was only about two miles from the bank, so it only took me a few minutes to get home.

The condominium building in which I lived was at the northeast corner of Willmore Park. There was an attractive fountain in front of the building. I pulled into the garage, then went upstairs to my second-floor condo.

When I opened the door to the condo, I noticed that my hands were shaking slightly. The incident at the bank had been very embarrassing, and I was badly rattled. Even though I had committed many crimes, no one had ever previously suspected me. It was humiliating to be treated like a criminal even though I was a criminal.

In order to calm my nerves, I poured myself a glass of wine and sat comfortably on the couch. I considered listening to some relaxing music, but I wasn't in the mood for music. I wanted to think about my predicament.

I realized that the FBI or police might show up to arrest me at any time. If they gathered a bit more circumstantial evidence, they might decide that they had enough evidence to bring charges against me.

One ace that I held up my sleeve was that I could always mindjack the judge. If my case went to trial, I could take control of the judge and dismiss all charges against me. However, that might attract a lot of attention, so I would prefer not to play that card.

Chapter 3
Hostage Rescue

For the next two days, I spent most of my time in my condo. I went once to the grocery store. In order to try to relax, I also took a couple of walks in the park behind the condominium building.

I usually followed the same path. First, I walked a lap around the small lake where fishermen seated in lawn chairs sought to catch trout and catfish. Then I headed up the hill upon whose summit there was a gazebo that was a popular site for family picnics. Although these family gatherings were pleasant to observe, I considered myself a "lone wolf" and didn't have any desire to be part of such a scenario.

For the next week, nothing happened, and I began to relax. Perhaps no charges would be brought against me.

I could understand the difficulty faced by the FBI, police, and prosecutors. They knew that I had committed the robberies, but they didn't understand how I had done so. They would look ridiculous if they tried to convince a jury that I had hypnotized employees at banks and jewelry stores. Even if law enforcement officials somehow realized that I had mindjacked those employees, it would be almost impossible to convince a jury that I had such an extraordinary power.

Although I was feeling safe from prosecution, I decided to end my life of crime. I had over two million dollars in savings and investments.

Just as I was becoming convinced that I would not hear from the FBI again, my telephone rang.

"Hello?" I answered.

"Hello, is this Andrew Preston?"

"Yes."

"Good afternoon, Mr. Preston. This is David Hummel with the FBI. We spoke at the bank last week."

"Yes, Agent Hummel. What can I do for you?"

He must have heard the tension in my voice because he said, "You can relax. I'm not calling about the robberies. This is a completely unrelated matter. It is a matter of great urgency, though. I am in downtown Clayton. There is a dangerous situation in a federal office building. A few minutes ago, it occurred to me that you could help us resolve this situation. Without your help, this could end badly."

"What's going on?"

"We have a hostage situation. An employee who was fired recently returned to his office two hours ago. He is heavily armed and is holding fifteen hostages. He has refused to speak with our negotiator. The situation inside the building seems to be getting worse, and we are concerned that he is going to start killing his hostages."

"That's unfortunate, but what does this have to do with me?"

"I don't know how you do the things that you do, but I'm hoping that you can help us. I give you my word that this isn't a trick or some attempt to entrap you. I am only interested in saving the lives of those persons in that office building."

I paused as I thought about what he had told me.

After a few seconds of silence, David asked, "Mr. Preston? Are you still there?"

"Yes. All right. I'll help."

"Thank you."

"What's the address?" I asked, reaching for my car keys.

"The police are sending a cruiser to pick you up. We need to get you here as soon as possible."

"Okay. I'll meet them in front of my building."

"Fine. I'll see you shortly."

After hanging up, I walked downstairs, through the lobby, and out the front door of my condo building. Shortly after I arrived at the curb on Jamieson Avenue, the police car pulled up, and I hopped inside.

With sirens blaring, we raced through several red lights. I held my breath at every intersection. Fortunately, the traffic yielded the right of way to the police car. Many persons even helped expedite our trip by pulling over to the side of the road.

We arrived in downtown Clayton much faster than I could have driven there in my own car. The police cruiser ride was also helpful because the officer took me directly to David Hummel. Without that help, it would have been difficult to find David in the crowd. Hundreds of persons had gathered on the street. Police barricades kept the crowd from getting too close to the office building.

After thanking the officer for the ride, I walked hurriedly over to David. We exchanged a quick handshake.

"Thank God, you're here!" he declared. "That guy inside could go ballistic at any moment!" He looked at me and added, "I don't know how close you need to be in order to hypnotize him or do whatever you do."

"I don't use hypnosis, but it would be helpful if I could see the gunman," I said.

David pointed toward the fourth floor. "He appears in that window occasionally. We have a sniper on the roof of a building across the street. However, the gunman always has his arm wrapped around the throat of a hostage. Our sniper can't get a clear shot."

"I don't need a clear shot," I said. "The next time that he appears in the window, I'll bring this situation to an end."

I believed that I could mindjack someone even without actually seeing the person, but I had never previously done so. This did not seem like a good occasion to try something like that for the first time.

After waiting nervously and impatiently for a couple of minutes, the gunman and his hostage appeared in the window. I could barely see the gunman, who stood behind the terrified woman.

It was sufficient, though. I instantly mindjacked the gunman. Looking through his eyes, I could see myself and David standing amongst the crowd on the street.

As my consciousness resided within the mind of this man, I was shocked by the chaos of his thoughts. In the cauldron of his mind, there was a poisonous brew of hatred, madness, jealously, fear, and rage.

I had never previously experienced such evil. It almost seemed demonic. I felt like I was contending with some external power for possession of his soul.

However, I was firmly in control. I walked away from the window. When I was halfway across the room and no longer within sight of the sniper, I forced the man to surrender. I released his grip on the woman, placed his gun on a table, and made him lay face down on the floor.

Within seconds, I felt him being seized by his former hostages. Since the man no longer posed a danger to anyone, I released him from the mindjack. I again saw through my own eyes as I stood on the sidewalk.

"The hostage situation is over," I told David. "At this moment, the man is being tied up by the persons that he held hostage."

"Are you certain?" David asked with wide eyes.

I grinned and nodded.

"Would you be willing to explain what you did?"

"No. However, I will tell you that you were wise to

call me. The gunman was planning to kill all those hostages. He only delayed because he wanted to get as much news coverage as possible."

"Thanks for your help," David said.

"You're welcome."

"I owe you," he added.

"Yes, you do."

David needed to remain on the scene for another two or three hours in order to speak with the prisoner and the former hostages. David arranged for a police officer to drive me home.

During the ride in the police cruiser, I reflected that it was now unlikely that I would ever be charged for any thefts. I realized that some FBI agents and police officials would not share David's gratitude for my help, so I could not yet completely relax. However, on the ride back to my condo, I felt good about the situation and about myself.

Chapter 4
National Security

Three days later, David Hummel stopped by my condo. We spoke for a few minutes about the hostage situation of earlier in the week, then David explained the main reason for his visit.

"The federal government needs your help," David told me. "There is a very serious threat from some terrorists who could wreak terrible harm on our country. We are willing to give you a complete pardon for all past crimes if you will come work for us."

"Are you kidding?"

"I couldn't be more serious. The paperwork for your pardon is being drafted as we speak."

"You want me to come work for the FBI?" I asked.

"Well, actually the NSA, the National Security Administration, wants to hire you. I have a friend in the NSA named Emma O'Connor. She works in a special, top secret division that recruits persons with abilities like yours. I don't understand how you do what you do, but Emma seems to understand."

"I doubt whether your friend, Emma, completely understands what I do, but I am intrigued by this job offer, and I am very pleased about the pardon."

"Keep in mind that this pardon will only cover all your past crimes until today," David cautioned. "It is not a license to do anything that you want. The pardon does not cover any future crimes."

"That's fine. I promise you that there won't be any future crimes. I'm placing that aspect of my life behind me. This new job might be a way for me to move forward in a positive way."

David had been watching me carefully. He smiled and nodded, apparently perceiving that my statement was sincere.

"Emma will be here any second. I asked her to wait in the car for a few minutes so that I could speak with you first. After she arrives, I'm going to go back down to the car so that she can speak with you privately."

"We NSA agents have a lot of secret stuff that we need to discuss privately," I grinned.

"I like your enthusiasm! And I hope this new job works out well for you."

"Thanks."

"Oh, here's Emma now," David said, looking over my shoulder.

I turned around to see an attractive blonde woman standing in the doorway. Although I had seen more beautiful women and had dated more beautiful women, she was certainly very nice looking.

"Hello, Mr. Preston. My name is Emma O'Connor. I'm a special agent with the NSA." She extended her right hand, and I shook hands with her.

She gave me a firm handshake, but she seemed rather delicate. I would have expected a special agent to have a vise-like grip.

"I explained to Andrew about the pardon and the job offer," David said. "He's very receptive to the idea."

"Good," Emma said. "I'm glad. We can use his help."

David headed toward the door. "I'll wait in the car. I have several calls to make so take as much time as you need."

"Thank you, David," Emma said as he left the condo.

"Would you like to sit down?" I asked, gesturing toward the couch.

"Yes."

I sat next to her on the couch.

"This is the first time that I've ever been offered a job without first needing to go to a job interview."

"Well, David is an old friend, and you made a good impression on him. I trust his judgment. However, I do have some concerns about your criminal past."

"I do have a criminal past, but there will be no criminal future."

"Hmmm. I hope that you are being truthful."

"I am," I said firmly.

"Well, we need your help. In fact, we are in desperate need of help. There are very few persons with your talent, so we were delighted when David found you."

"What exactly is my talent?"

"You don't know?" she asked with a smile.

"I know, but I doubt that you and David know."

"You are a telepath who can take control of the minds of other persons. You can compel persons to do anything that you want, and you can read their thoughts."

My eyes widened. "Apparently, I was wrong. You do know what I can do."

She nodded. "We are willing to take a chance on

you because you have such a rare and useful talent."

"I'll try not to disappoint you."

"Please don't. I will be very unhappy if mysterious, unexplainable robberies begin occurring in Maryland near our NSA offices."

I sighed. "You don't need to worry about that happening. I know that it was wrong to commit those robberies. However, anyone who had my powers would succumb to temptation. Anyone would use their powers to profit themselves."

"Would they?"

"Yes, they would. You have no idea what it is like to possess power like mine."

"It must be awesome," Emma said.

"It is."

"I can only imagine what it must be like." She looked at me critically.

"And I can tell that you are judging me."

"Are you reading my mind?" she asked.

"No, I'm reading your face," I replied. "You have a very expressive face."

"Is it good for me to have an expressive face?" Emma asked.

"It's okay, but you wouldn't be a good poker player. Everyone playing poker against you would be able tell how strong a hand you held."

"Fortunately, I don't play poker," she said.

She was silent for a few seconds and seemed to be studying my face.

"Why are you looking at me that way?" I asked.

"You need a shave."

"Oh, really?"

"Yes. What exactly is the purpose of that five-day growth beard?"

"It suits my style."

"Since you're a thief, a beard can be useful. After your image has been recorded by surveillance cameras, you can change your appearance simply by shaving your beard."

"Yes. We thieves find beards to be quite helpful."

"That's nice." She continued to study my face. "You also need a haircut. Is long hair part of your chameleon-like disguise?"

"No. I just look good with long hair."

"Do you think so?" she asked demurely.

"Wow! Is there anything else wrong with my

appearance?"

"Your eyebrows could use some work."

I laughed. "Are you a special agent or a cosmetologist?"

"I am a multi-faceted woman, and you are a multi-faceted man. You project one image to the world, but I can tell that there is much more to you."

"That almost sounds like a compliment."

"Not necessarily."

"You dislike me, don't you?"

"I dislike that you're a thief. You're a thief with a full pardon, but you're still a thief."

"I'm not as bad as you think that I am. A lot of the money that I stole I gave away to charity."

"It wasn't your money to give away."

"That's true," I acknowledged.

"And seven persons were fired as a result of your thefts," she added. "Three jewelry stores clerks, and four bank employees were fired. Some were fired for being careless. Others were suspected of being involved in the thefts. No one was prosecuted, but you damaged their reputations."

"I didn't intend to harm anyone. I'm sorry."

"There's no need to apologize to me. You haven't done anything to me."

"Well, I'm sorry that I harmed them."

"Actions have consequences, Mr. Preston."

"Yes."

She stood up. "It's been nice to meet you, but I need to be on my way. We'll be in touch with you again soon."

"When?"

"Probably tomorrow," she said, heading for the door. "Goodbye."

"Bye."

After her somewhat hasty departure, I sat back down on the couch and reflected upon the conversation. It occurred to me that I should have asked her more questions about this job that the NSA was offering to me.

To my surprise, I realized that it bothered me that I had inadvertently caused seven persons to be fired. I felt guilty about what I had done.

I also was bothered that Emma O'Connor had such a bad opinion of me. For some mysterious reason, I wanted her to like and respect me.

Within a few minutes, I decided to take some

positive, proactive steps toward reducing my guilt and improving Emma O'Connor's opinion of me. I picked up my phone and called my lawyer.

The next afternoon, I walked through the lobby and out the front doors of my condominium building. As I headed toward my car, which was parked on the street, I heard someone calling my name. I turned around to see Emma hurrying toward me.

"Mr. Preston!"

"Hello, Miss O'Connor," I said.

"You are obviously on your way out," she said as she approached me. "I should have called first."

"That's okay. I was just going to the grocery store. It can wait."

"Good," she smiled. Emma glanced at the fountain by which we were standing. "I like the dancing waters patterns of this fountain."

"Yes, I like it, too. After dark, the fountain is illuminated by some multi-colored lights."

"This will be a nice place for us to talk," Emma said, sitting down on the bench by the fountain.

"I'm looking forward to starting this job with this

NSA," I said as I joined her on the bench.

"Oh, why are you looking forward to the job?"

"It will be interesting to use my powers in new ways. I also like the idea of helping my country."

"Are you a patriotic person?" she asked.

"About average, I suppose."

She frowned at me. This woman was certainly difficult to please.

"Mr. Preston, I hope that you understand that you have accepted a dangerous job. You'll need more than an average level of patriotism in order to meet the challenges of this job."

"Okay."

"Are you willing to give your life for your country?"

"You sure ask a lot of questions," I said. "You are like a psychologist. Psychologists ask one question after another in order to get the patient talking about himself."

"Have you been to a psychologist?"

"And yet another question! In answer to that question, no, I have not been to a psychologist. Everything that I know about them is from television shows and movies."

"I would suppose that some psychologists ask a lot

of questions and others don't," she said.

"You're probably right," I acknowledged.

"And you're right that I do ask a lot of questions," Emma said. "It was a technique that I learned in law school. It is called 'the Socratic method.' One question leads to the next question to the next question. The Socratic method is a means of discerning the truth."

"You went to law school?" I asked.

"Yes. I was an FBI agent before I joined the NSA."

"Why did you change jobs?"

"That is a long story for another day."

"I'll look forward to hearing that story," I said.

"You never answered my question about whether you are willing to give your life for your country."

"I suppose that we will find out when the time comes."

"Yes, we will. I'm not optimistic, though. You have been living a very selfish life. There is no reason to believe that you will be willing to sacrifice yourself."

"Am I going to be lectured?"

"No. You are being presented with an opportunity. I am giving you a chance to leave behind your selfish life and to transcend yourself. I offer you the opportunity to serve a higher and noble cause."

"Thanks."

"Is that all you have to say?"

"Will this job with the NSA pay me a salary?" I asked.

She stared at me. "Is there no limit to your greed? Do you ever stop thinking about money? You are a millionaire. What do you care about receiving a government paycheck?"

"I'm no longer a millionaire. I reimbursed the banks and jewelry stores for the money that I stole. I also gave a lot of money to the seven persons who got fired."

Her expression softened. "Why did you do such a thing?"

"Actions have consequences. Someone that I know told me that not too long ago. I wanted to do something good in order to bring about some good consequences."

"Hmmm." She looked reflective.

"What?"

"I would not have expected you to do what you did."

"I'm a bundle of surprises."

"Making restitution was a good thing to do, Andrew."

It was the first time that she had called me by my

first name. I was surprised by how much I relished the moment.

"Thank you," I said simply.

"In answer to your question about whether the NSA will pay you, you will receive a salary. You'll be issued a photo ID card and will be an employee of the NSA. You might eventually get your own office."

"Well, office or no office, the job is intriguing. This will be a great adventure."

"Welcome aboard," Emma smiled and shook hands with me.

I was happy that she seemed pleased that I would be working with her.

"I hope that you're not completely broke," she said as we stood up and began strolling along the sidewalk.

"Oh, no. I have worked at several actual jobs so I kept the money that I saved from those jobs. In the last five years, I've also made some good investments, so I'm keeping that money, too."

"Will you be able to keep your condo?" she asked.

"Yes, I plan to keep it for a while. Do I need to relocate to Maryland for this new job?"

"Well, we are going to need you to come to

Maryland for a few weeks. We need to train you and get you started on your first project. However, our psy-ops unit is pretty flexible. You might be able to work remotely in St. Louis and just come to Maryland when necessary."

"Telecommuting for telepaths?" I quipped.

She laughed. "I suppose so. You can discuss those details with your supervisor when you meet him. Can you be ready to leave tomorrow?"

"Yes, that will be fine."

"Good. We'll be flying to Baltimore. The NSA headquarters are in Fort Meade, Maryland. However, our unit is located a few miles away from headquarters."

After conversing for a couple of more minutes about the details of my trip to Maryland, Emma and I said goodbye. After she got in her car and drove away, I started to walk toward my own car. However, then I decided that I did not need to buy any groceries since I'd be leaving for Maryland in the morning. Instead of going to the store, I went back up into my condo and started packing.

Chapter 5

Night of the Assassins

Although I am usually a "night owl," I went to bed before midnight since I was going to have to get up so early in the morning. I set the alarm on my cell phone for 5:30 a.m., then placed the phone on the nightstand by my bed. Just as I was drifting off to sleep, the phone rang.

"Hello?" I answered groggily.

"Andrew, this is David Hummel. You have to get out of your condo as quickly as possible! Several FBI agents and I are on the way to your building, but we won't be there for a while."

"What's going on?"

"The NSA just contacted the FBI about an encrypted message that they intercepted and decoded. NSA computer experts hacked an encrypted email account being used by some terrorists whom the NSA has been tracking. Based upon a new email message, both the NSA and the FBI think that a hit team is heading toward your condo building!"

"You have to be kidding." I was now fully awake,

but I could not believe what I was hearing. "That seems highly unlikely, David."

"Listen carefully!" he insisted. "You are in danger! You must leave immediately! Don't go near your car. Run into the park and hide there."

The urgent tone of his voice as well as the imminent danger spurred me to action. I jumped out of bed, slipped on some jeans, and some loafers. Still holding my phone, I went out the bedroom door with the intention of leaving my condo.

However, as soon as I stepped into the living room, I realized that it was too late to get out of the condo. There were persons on the balcony, and their faces were pressed against the glass of the balcony doors.

I ducked behind a chair, hoping that they had not seen me. The balcony doors could be locked, but since I was on the second floor, I seldom bothered locking them. As I crouched behind the chair, I silently reprimanded myself for not properly securing my condo.

The balcony doors burst open. Two men dressed in black wearing night vision goggles stepped off the balcony into my condo. The men held guns equipped with silencers.

As their eyes scanned the room, one man spotted me peeking out from behind the chair. He started to aim his gun at me, but he was unable to complete the move. I mindjacked him quickly and forcefully.

Completely in control of him, I turned his gun toward the other assassin and shot the man in the right shoulder. I could just as easily have shot him in the head, but I decided to be merciful. In all likelihood, the man would survive the bullet wound in his shoulder.

It was, though, a serious wound. The man dropped his gun and collapsed onto the carpet. With his left hand, he clutched his shoulder.

Since I was being merciful, I also spared the life of the second man. Instead of having him shoot himself in the head, I forced him to toss his gun toward me, then run back outside onto the balcony and jump over the railing.

From this second-floor balcony, the man fell onto the muddy ground below. I felt his hip break, but that was the only major injury that he sustained. I released him from my control.

I picked up my cell phone. "I'm okay. Two armed men entered my condo, but I have disabled both of them. They are no longer a threat to me."

"Keep your lights off and stay hidden!" David exclaimed. "They would not send only two men. There are likely more attackers nearby."

"Okay."

I picked up both guns, then sat with my back against the wall. If any more assassins came into the room, I would probably just mindjack them, too, but it was good to have the guns as a backup. Either through chemical conditioning or innate ability, it was possible that some assassins could resist being mindjacked. I might have to use a gun to stop someone who could not be mindjacked.

"Our ETA is five minutes," David said on the phone.

It took me a few seconds to recall that ETA was an acronym for "estimated time of arrival." Although five minutes is a short period of time, in the present circumstances, it would seem like a long time.

I noticed that man with the shoulder wound was slowly crawling across the floor. I realized that he might have a second gun and be planning to shoot me. Without hesitation, I mindjacked him. As soon as I was in his mind, I felt the awful pain from the wound. He did not have a second gun. The man had a knife, but he was in no condition to attack me. He was close to going into shock from the wound.

Just before I released the man from the mindjacking, I placed him into a deep sleep. I started to move across the room so that I could get a better view of the balcony and the backyard.

The mirror on the wall behind me shattered. I was startled and dropped flat onto the carpet. That bullet had narrowly missed me.

There was no one on the balcony, so I knew that the shooter had to be somewhere in the park. I had never previously mindjacked someone who I could not see, but I believed that I could do so.

I allowed my thoughts to drift outside across the balcony, down into the backyard, and out into the park that bordered the building. My consciousness moved over the dark, almost empty park. I felt a few blips of energy that radiated some small degree of a basic, simple intelligence. I was certain that they were merely animals in the park, probably birds and squirrels.

Then, as my thoughts went deeper into the park and up a hillside, I came upon a human intelligence. I seized the man's mind, and all of his thoughts belonged to me.

Looking through his eyes and through the scope of his rifle, I could see into my condo. When I stood up, I could see myself directly in the crosshairs of the night vision scope. Even for me, it was a very strange experience.

I probed the sniper's thoughts and soon found the information that I wanted. There was a fourth man waiting in a car. I rendered the sniper unconscious, then moved my thoughts toward the street where the driver sat in an SUV. I mindjacked him and obtained some additional insights about their plot against me.

"Hello, David," I spoke into my cell phone. "I just knocked out a sniper on a hill in the park and the driver of their vehicle. There is a silver SUV parked on Jamieson Avenue near the playground. The driver is armed, but he will still be asleep when you get here."

"Were those the only four men?"

"Yes."

"Okay. We'll be there in about a minute."

His time estimate was very accurate. In just over a minute, there was a loud knocking on the door. I walked over and opened the door. As David and two other men came inside, I switched on the lights.

"Are you okay?" David asked.

"Yes, I'm fine." I pointed at the unconscious, wounded attacker. "However, he is in urgent need of medical attention."

"We have a medical team on the way."

"There's also a man outside who is going to need medical help. I forced him to throw himself over the balcony. He has a broken hip."

"Yes. We saw him on the ground. However, we haven't yet located the sniper."

"I can show you where the sniper is," I volunteered.

"Good. Show us."

I walked outside with David and another FBI agent.

"Does Emma know what has happened?" I asked.

"Yes," David replied. "I called her while we were on the way here. After we've secured this location, I'll call her back and give her an update."

"Is Emma going to come here tonight?" I asked.

"Well, she's on her way back to St. Louis from Lake Lotawana, which is near Kansas City. The NSA found another potential recruit at Lake Lotawana, so Emma made a quick trip there. She'll be back in St. Louis in the morning."

"Oh, okay."

David, the other FBI agent, and I walked past the small lake, then ascended a hill upon whose summit was the gazebo that was a popular spot for picnics. The sniper lay unconscious on the floor of the gazebo.

While David examined the sniper's rifle, the other FBI agent handcuffed the man. Within a few minutes, more FBI agents arrived at the scene. David and I returned to my condo.

"I don't expect any more trouble tonight, but I'm going to assign two agents to stay here until you leave for Maryland tomorrow."

"Thanks. I'll sleep better knowing that I have some bodyguards nearby."

After conversing with David for a few more minutes, he departed, and I went to bed and soon fell asleep.

Chapter 6
Emma's Tale

When I woke up in the morning, I rolled over and glanced at the clock on the nightstand. It was almost ten o'clock. I was surprised because I seldom slept that late.

After showering and getting dressed, I walked out of the bedroom. One of the agents was seated on the couch as he typed a text message on his phone. The other agent was outside on the balcony. He was looking toward the street.

This agent stepped back inside. "Miss O'Connor just parked and is heading this way," he told me and the other agent.

"Yeah, I know," the second agent said. "I was just texting with her."

After speaking briefly to the two agents, I went across the room and opened the front door just as she was approaching it.

"Good morning," I greeted her.

"Good morning, sleepyhead," she said. "A little bird told me that you just got up."

"Hmmm. I can guess the identity of that little bird," I said, glancing back at the agent who had been exchanging text messages with her.

A guilty grin appeared on that man's face, and he shrugged.

I turned back toward her. "I usually get up earlier. I don't know why I was so tired."

"You were so tired because you used your powers so much last night," she explained. "And you used those powers in ways that you had never previously used them."

"That's true," I acknowledged. "I did expend a lot of energy."

"Other telepaths have experienced the same thing," she said. "Every time that someone uses power in a new way, that person needs more sleep. Using telepathic powers also makes persons very hungry sometimes."

"Now that you mention it, I am rather hungry." I looked toward the kitchen. "At the moment, I don't have much food here."

"I'll take you out to breakfast," she said.

"That sounds like a good idea," I enthusiastically accepted her invitation.

"Gentlemen, if you hold down the fort here while

we're gone, I promise to bring you back some carryout sandwiches," she told the two agents, who quickly agreed.

"I'm certainly glad that the computer experts at the NSA were able to intercept that email message sent between the terrorist groups. If David's phone call had not awakened me, those two men would have shot me to death while I was sleeping."

Emma nodded. "Yes, it was fortunate that you received the warning in time. If you had been killed, I would have blamed myself for not providing you with adequate security."

"It wouldn't have been your fault. No one could anticipate that the terrorists would come to kill a brand new NSA employee who hadn't even started work yet."

"That is puzzling," Emma agreed. "We are very concerned about how they found out about you so quickly. I need to tell you some top-secret information now. A few weeks ago, Rachel Kolbe, one of our analysts … and my friend … was killed by a telepathic attack that caused her to have a stroke."

"That's awful! I'm sorry for your loss."

"Yes, thank you. Rachel was a wonderful person. And brilliant. Our director had assigned her the task of finding the traitor within our unit. For various reasons, we're sure that we've been infiltrated. I'll tell you more details later today."

"Okay."

"I'm confident that we'll eventually find the infiltrator."

"Hopefully soon."

"Yes."

Emma and I went to a nearby diner that was popular with residents in my neighborhood. We sat in a booth by the window and watched the late morning traffic.

"Last night David mentioned that you went to speak with a potential new recruit at Lake Lotawana. Did you have a lot of luck at Lotawana?" I punned.

"I saw a lot of lovely scenery at Lotawana and a lot of pretty sailboats, but I didn't find any telepaths. The potential recruit was a very good magician who used sleight of hand for his magic tricks. He has no telepathic abilities at all."

"Oh, that's too bad."

She shrugged. "He was not the first magician who has been mistaken for a telepath. In fact, most of our potential recruits turn out not to have any telepathic abilities. You are the most powerful telepath that we have ever found."

"Thanks."

"I'm simply stating a fact."

The diner was still serving its breakfast menu, so Emma and I ordered some scrambled eggs and toast. I took a sip from a glass of milk while I watched Emma butter a slice of toast.

"I'm surprised that you invited me to breakfast. I thought that you hated me."

"I barely know you. I certainly don't hate you."

"Good."

"I don't hate anyone," she said. "I hate the things that some persons do, but I try not to hate the persons themselves. I'll admit, though, that it's difficult not to hate terrorists."

"I feel the same way. I'm looking forward to using my abilities against the terrorists. I'd like to destroy as many terrorist groups as I can."

"You will have that opportunity. I, too, want to take the fight to the enemy. However, at the moment, we are on the defensive. The NSA believes that the terrorists have found some telepaths and formed a group of terrorist telepaths. These terrorist telepaths could wreak terrible harm in our country and throughout the world."

"Why does the NSA believe that this terrorist telepathic group exists?" I asked.

"For the past year, the NSA has intercepted numerous Internet communications that indicated that the group was being formed. Then, in recent weeks, there have been several incidents in which United States diplomats, military officers, and CIA agents were apparently mindjacked."

"Why do you believe that they were mindjacked?"

"The first incident occurred several weeks ago in Turkey. The CIA station chief went on a shooting rampage in which he killed and wounded many persons before he was shot to death by a CIA agent. At first, everyone thought that this was just another of those unfortunate mass shootings that occurs from time to time. This station chief was in good standing with the CIA, and he had never previously shown any signs of instability, but mental illness sometimes goes undetected. However, shortly after this tragic event, the NSA decoded messages that we had intercepted. Those Internet messages revealed the existence of the terrorist telepaths and their mindjacking of the CIA station chief. One week later, at an embassy in France, the ambassador emailed top-secret documents to a known terrorist operative. The ambassador sent the documents from the computer on the desk in his office, but he has no recollection of having done so. There have been a few other incidents, too. Based upon some terrorist communications that we intercepted last week, we anticipate that things will soon get much worse."

I briefly reflected upon this information. "I have always wondered whether there were other telepaths around with the ability to mindjack persons. Apparently, there are, and some of them are working for the bad guys."

"Fortunately, some of them are also working for us. There could be a full-scale war between telepaths that will affect the fate of millions of persons."

"I will like using my abilities for a good cause," I said. "My behavior over the last few years has been totally unacceptable. Greed was probably my main motivation for mindjacking those persons at the banks and jewelry stores. However, I also enjoy having such special powers, and I want to use those powers."

"You enjoy mindjacking persons," Emma said.

"Yes," I admitted.

"Well, you've been given a gift, so it's natural that you would want to use it. Have you mindjacked me?"

"No, I haven't."

"Have you tried to mindjack me?" she asked.

"No."

"Are you sure that you could mindjack me if you tried to do so?"

"I suppose that I could," I replied.

"Why do you think so?"

"Well, I have been able to mindjack everyone that I have tried to mindjack."

"Why haven't you tried to mindjack me?"

"I don't mindjack people that I know personally."

"Why not?"

"It would be disrespectful." I hesitated, then continued, "It seems like a violation of the other person. I was wrong to mindjack those persons at the banks and jewelry stores. I didn't know them personally, but it was still disrespectful to mindjack them."

Emma looked at me intently. "You're becoming a better person, Andrew."

"Well, I'm trying. I still have a long way to go."

"I'm curious whether you could mindjack me," she

said. "Go ahead. Try to mindjack me."

"No."

"I give you permission. Do it."

"No."

"Look at it from this perspective: we're on the same psy-ops team now, and we need to understand each other's abilities. I want to gain a better understanding of your telepathic strength, and I need to practice blocking telepaths from taking control of my mind. What if one of the terrorist telepaths tried to mindjack me today? Perhaps I could learn to resist being mindjacked."

"All right," I agreed reluctantly, persuaded by the logic of her statement. "Tell me when you're ready for me to begin."

"I'm ready," Emma said. "Go ahead."

I looked her in the eyes and allowed my consciousness to envelope her. I experienced a cool, calm, pleasantness. It must be nice to be this person for 24 hours a day. Within me, an inner war was raging, but this woman was at peace with herself.

For a few seconds, I savored my union with her calm spirit. Then a steel wall slammed into place, and her mind was closed to me.

I was startled, and my arms flailed outwards, knocking over my glass of milk.

"Is something wrong?" she asked with a grin.

"How did you do that?"

"Do what?" She looked at me with feigned innocence.

"You blocked me out of your mind. I didn't know that anyone could block me."

"I'm not anyone. I'm an agent with the NSA's psy-ops division."

"What telepathic powers do you have?" I asked.

"That information is top secret." With a napkin, she wiped up the milk that I had spilt on the table.

"Can you mindjack people?" I persisted.

"That information is very top secret."

"So confide in me. Since I'm now working for the NSA, I'd assume that I have top-secret security clearance."

"When we get to Maryland, I'll tell you more about what I can do." Emma stood up. "We'd probably better head back to your condo so that you can finish packing."

"Okay." I could tell that Emma was not going to reveal any more secrets to me this morning. This seemed like a good time for me to reveal some information that I had gleaned last night. “Did you ever hear of a group called ‘the Jinn’?” I asked.

“I recall from a college class in folklore that Jinn are genies. Why do you ask?”

“Last night, when I probed the mind of one of the hit men, he was thinking about the Jinn. The terrorist telepaths apparently call themselves ‘the Jinn.’ I had the impression that the order to kill me had come from them. The Jinn work as mercenaries for terrorist groups.”

“Oh, wow!”

“The hit man didn’t know much about the Jinn. He didn’t even know in what country they reside. Most of the field operatives like those hit men don’t have any telepathic abilities. They just carry out the orders that they receive.”

“Good work, Andrew,” Emma said. “That information will be very helpful.”

Before we left the diner, Emma purchased two sandwiches for the FBI agents who were back at my condo.

When we got back to the condo, the two agents were pleased that she had remembered to bring them sandwiches. I got them two cans of soda from my refrigerator.

While they ate, Emma used her NSA phone to transmit an encrypted text message to the director of her psy-ops unit. Emma wanted to inform the NSA about what I had learned from probing the mind of the hit man.

After sending the text message, Emma helped me complete packing, and we managed to squeeze everything into one small suitcase.

"Are you sure that you're bringing enough clothing?" Emma asked. "It might be a while before you're able to return to St. Louis."

"I like to travel light. In a few days, I'll buy some more clothes and anything else that I need."

When Emma and I left for the airport, the two agents returned to their local FBI office. Upon arriving at Lambert Field, Emma returned her rental car. The airport was not crowded, and we passed through security without any delays.

Soon we boarded the plane bound for Baltimore, Maryland. Emma sat in a window seat, and I sat next to her. I was glad that no one sat in the aisle seat because it gave me more room and allowed Emma and me to speak more freely. An elderly couple sat in the row behind us, and a young couple with a little boy were in the row in front of us.

As Emma and I conversed during the flight, I kept my voice very low even though I was confident that no one within hearing range was eavesdropping on us.

"I'm looking forward to seeing the Information Dominance Center," I said. "I recall reading that the room was designed to look like the bridge of the Starship Enterprise. I want to sit in Captain Jean-Luc Picard's chair."

"Unfortunately, that operations center is not at our facility, so it might be a while before you get to see it. Through the years, the room has been modified quite a lot, so it no longer closely resembles the bridge of the Starship Enterprise."

"The article that I read said that the doors to the room make a whooshing sound when they slide open and closed," I continued undeterred.

"Yes, they do. It is kind of a cool room. When we visit that facility, I'll make sure that you get to go into the control room, Andrew."

"Thanks."

After landing in Baltimore and disembarking from

the plane, Emma and I had made a quick trip through the terminal. Since we had both brought carry-on luggage, it was not necessary for us to wait at a baggage carrousel. We headed directly to the airport's parking garage and went to her car.

"I'm sure that you'd like to get settled into your new apartment before we go to work," Emma said as she drove along the access road leading to the highway.

"Yes, thanks."

"Your apartment is only about three miles from our campus. The NSA rents three apartments in that building."

"Do you live in that apartment building?"

"No, but my apartment is only a short distance away. It's within walking distance of your place."

"Good." I glanced at the map on my cell phone. "Will we be going to the Fort Meade headquarters today?"

"Not today. In fact, we probably won't go there this month. Those of us in the psy-ops unit seldom go to the Fort Meade headquarters. When we need to have a meeting with NSA personnel at headquarters, we usually have a videoconference over encrypted Internet lines. In our meeting room and in the Fort Meade headquarters, there are huge, wall-sized, high-resolution screens for videoconferencing."

"Videoconferencing is usually just as good as meeting in person," I said.

"Yes. In addition to the convenience and efficiency of teleconferencing, we hope that teleconferencing helps keep our identities secret. We are sure that the Fort Meade headquarters is under observation by our enemies. They might be photographing and identifying persons who go in and out of NSA headquarters. We hope that our enemies are unaware of our small, secret campus."

Upon arriving at the apartment building, I was pleased to see that it reminded me of my condominium building in St. Louis. After Emma parked, we walked across the lawn past some azalea bushes. Two purple martins flew past us.

"Even the birds are glad that you're here, Andrew."

"Since we're so near Baltimore, shouldn't it be orioles that are welcoming me?" I asked.

"I'm sure that some orioles will be flying by soon."

"Good."

We went up to the third floor and into the apartment where I would be staying. The apartment was smaller than my condo, but it still looked like it would be a comfortable place for me to live. I liked the granite countertop in the kitchenette.

Emma opened the refrigerator door. “There’s not much in here. Later today, on the way back from our NSA campus, we can stop by a store and buy some groceries for you.”

“I appreciate all your help, Emma.” I sat down on the couch. When Emma joined me on the couch, I looked at her intently and asked, “Well?”

“Well what?”

“We’re in Maryland,” I said.

“It’s hard to slip anything past you, Andrew.”

“This morning at the diner, you said that when we got to Maryland, you would tell me more about what you could do telepathically.”

Emma chuckled. “Have you been waiting all day to find out what I can do?”

“Yes,” I answered honestly.

“Such patience deserves a true answer,” Emma said. “Yes, I am a telepath. My abilities are similar to yours, although I think that you are more powerful.”

“I might not be. You were able to block me from your mind.”

"It's easier to defend your own mind than it is to take control of someone else's mind," she said.

"That's true."

"I'm wondering whether I could mindjack you. Would it be okay with you if I tried?"

"Sure. You can try," I smirked.

Emma smiled sweetly. "Good. I think that I'll make you do the hokey pokey."

"Go for it," I challenged her.

Like an ocean wave, her mental energy swept over me. To my horror, I began to put my right hand in. Within seconds, she would have me putting my right hand out, turning myself around, and doing the entire hokey pokey sequence of dance-like moves.

I slammed a shield into place. It was a reflexive action to the threat of losing control. Emma tried to break through the shield, and she almost succeeded. The shield held, though, and I relaxed.

"Darn! I thought that I had you," Emma said.

"For a few seconds, you did. I underestimated you. I won't make that mistake again."

"You should have let me take control. You would have had fun doing the hokey pokey."

"Because that's what it's all about," I joked.

"Right," she grinned.

"How did you become a NSA agent, Emma?"

"Until two years ago, I was an FBI agent. My primary assignment was stopping online scams. Some of those criminals stole many thousands of dollars from their victims. I would set up a sting operation in which I would pretend to be a potential victim. After making initial contact online, I would eventually talk on the phone to the scammer. As soon as the conversation began, I would mindjack the criminal. Then I would force him to drive to the nearest FBI office, turn himself in, and confess."

"You can mindjack someone to whom you are speaking on the phone?" I asked.

"Yes," she replied.

"I'm impressed!"

"Have you ever tried?" she asked.

"No."

"You probably can do it, too."

"I'm looking forward to trying."

"Like Nathaniel, I kept quiet about my telepathic abilities. There were only three persons in the FBI who knew what I could do. David Hummel was one of those three. I worked with David on several cases. I liked him and trusted him, and he proved himself worthy of my trust."

"David seems like a good guy."

Emma nodded. "Yes, he is. Two years ago the NSA quietly put out word that they were looking for persons with telepathic ability. The NSA was forming a special psy-ops unit, and they were looking for recruits. This assignment seemed like a perfect fit for me. I went over to NSA headquarters and was interviewed by Nathaniel. Nathaniel offered me the job, so I resigned from the FBI and joined the NSA. David Hummel knew that we needed additional persons for our team. When you manifested your powers, he contacted me about you."

Emma's phone chirped to signal that she had received a text message. "I'm sorry for this interruption," she said as she looked at the phone's screen.

"That's okay. It might be important."

After quickly reading the message, she said, "It was important. Two of the four men who tried to kill you at your condo have been brought here to Maryland so that they can be interrogated."

"I'd assume that they will be interrogating the sniper

and the driver since they weren't injured."

"That's right. The other two men will be all right, but they are still in St. Louis. They'll be brought to Maryland in a couple of days. In the meantime, I'm sure that we'll get some useful information from the driver and the sniper. FBI and NSA agents will be speaking with them."

"Will you be speaking with them?" I asked.

"Yes. I'm scheduled to interrogate them tomorrow morning. Actually, I doubt that there will be much talking. In all likelihood, I will simply mindjack them and obtain as much information as I can."

I nodded. "That would be the most logical way to do it. If you interrogate them, they will either say nothing or tell you lies."

"We have a report that some enemy operatives are being chemically conditioned to resist mindjacking. Since you were able to enter the minds of these four men last night, apparently they have not been conditioned to resist."

"Or else I'm just so great at mindjacking that I broke through their excellent conditioning," I said with a smile.

She returned the smile. "That's possible. You do have excellent skills."

“Thank you. Hopefully, if the time comes when I need to do so, I will be able to break through any chemical defenses. I did not detect any resistance in those four men, though. If any chemical conditioning was done to them, it was done very poorly.”

“I suppose that was the first time that you ever mindjacked four persons in the same day,” she said.

“Yes. Two persons was my previous record. Admittedly, it is a rather pathetic record.”

She laughed. “No, it’s not! Only a handful of persons in the world can do what we can do. Your abilities are awesome!”

“Well, I’m certainly glad to be here and putting my abilities to good use. We’re like sentinels guarding the gates against the forces of evil.”

“We’re mental sentinels,” Emma quipped, then stood up. “We’d better get going.”

We walked downstairs and went outside toward her car.

“Before we go to the NSA campus, I should tell you about a tragic event that occurred five months ago. One of our apprentices, Stacey Nolan, died of a cocaine overdose. Her death was especially troubling because of the suspicious circumstances. At that time, I suspected that someone forced her to take the drug overdose. However, since Rachel Kolbe's recent murder, I'm now sure that Stacey was murdered, too."

"So you think that Stacey was mindjacked?"

Emma nodded. "Someone could have mindjacked her and forced her to take cocaine. Perhaps, like Rachel, Stacey discovered the identity of the traitor within the NSA."

Emma and I continued to discuss this subject as we headed toward our destination.

Chapter 7

Nathaniel's Tale

It was a short, scenic drive to the NSA campus. Along the way, we passed several attractive groves of cherry blossom trees and crabapple trees.

Upon arriving at our destination, I found that it did indeed resemble a college campus. However, unlike most colleges, everyone had to drive through a security gate in order to enter the campus.

After Emma showed her identification card to the security officer at the gate, she drove down the lane and found a parking spot. We got out of the car and began a leisurely walk across the campus.

I liked the small lake and the ornamental bridge that spanned a narrow section of the lake. It reminded me of a similar bridge in the Japanese garden that was in the Missouri Botanical Gardens.

Emma and I went into the main building and headed down a hallway toward the offices of the psy-ops unit. We arrived at a classroom whose glass wall allowed us to see everyone and everything inside. Several men and women sat in chairs arranged in a semi-circle in front of a woman who appeared to be the teacher.

We paused to watch the class.

"Those are our apprentice telepaths," Emma explained. "Julie Constant is teaching the class. If you weren't so darn powerful, you'd be placed in that apprentice class."

"I'm so cool it's unbelievable," I said jokingly.

"Yeah, right."

Julie Constant noticed us observing the class and waved for us to come into the room. Emma greeted Julie and the apprentices, then introduced me to the group.

"This is Andrew Preston. He's the newest member of our team. Andrew has some excellent skills, and I'm sure all of us will enjoy working with him."

After Julie and the apprentices made some nice comments to welcome me, Julie introduced the apprentices to me.

"All of our apprentices have traveled very different roads to get here," Julie said, walking over to stand behind the chairs in which two women in their mid-twenties were seated. "Andrew, I'd like for you to meet Leslie and

Becca. We call these two the 'Minnesota twins' because they're both from Minneapolis."

"And because we both have red hair," Leslie said.

"And we went to the same college, but we never met until we started working here," Becca added.

Julie gestured toward a slender young man with an intense expression. "Bryan is a multi-talented member of our team. He is a computer expert who was recruited by the NSA cyber-security data center, and he later transferred over to our psy-ops unit."

"We're fortunate to have a technical wizard in our unit," Leslie said.

"Yes, whenever I have a problem with my laptop or tablet, Bryan knows what to do in order to fix it," Becca said.

"I'm always happy to help if I can," Bryan said.

"This is Kristy," Emma said, placing her hand on the shoulder of a pretty, petite woman with a wide smile. "Like you, Kristy is from Missouri."

"Missouri seems to be a great place to find telepaths," Julie said.

"Perhaps there is something in the water of the Mississippi River," I suggested.

"Maybe," Julie laughed.

"Kristy has something else in common with you, Andrew," Emma said. "Like you, she has rescued hostages."

"Oh, that's great. What happened, Kristy?" I asked.

"Last year, at my son's school, some psycho came into the teachers' lounge while I was speaking with my son's teacher. At that time, there were four other teachers in the lounge eating lunch. Anyway, to make a long story short, I mindjacked the psycho and forced him to give me his gun. Nobody got hurt."

"The weird thing is that this was the first time that Kristy ever used telepathic power," Julie said. "Before that day, she had no idea that she had any telepathic powers."

"The crisis forced you to find the power to do what you needed to do," Becca said.

"Necessity is the mother of invention," Julie quoted.

"I've often heard that quote. Who said it first?" Becca asked.

"Plato wrote that quote in Greek in his book **The Republic**," Julie said.

"Necessity was also the catalyst for the manifestation of my powers," Ronnie said, joining the conversation. "However, I did not rescue any hostages. In fact, the need that caused my powers to bloom was not admirable at all. Due to too much partying, I was failing all of my college classes. I was on the verge of being kicked out of the university. Then, one morning while I was sitting in class taking a test for which I was unprepared, I began to pick up the thoughts of my classmates. I plucked the test answers from their minds. I got an A on an exam that I should have failed."

"Cool. I wish that I could have done that when I was in college," Becca said.

"It was very helpful," Ronnie continued. "As result of my newfound power, I got good grades in all my classes by reading the minds of the other students and the professors. It wasn't an admirable way for me to discover my telepathic powers. I suppose that I'm the bad boy in this group."

"Did you rob any banks or jewelry stores?" I asked.

"Would you look at the time?" Emma interrupted the conversation in order to cut me off. "Nathaniel will be waiting for us, Andrew. We're supposed to be in his office right now." She took hold of my elbow and propelled me toward the door.

"It was very nice to meet all of you," I told the group.

"Nice to meet you, too, Andrew,"

"I look forward to working with you," Julie Constant said.

"See you later," Kristy said as Emma and I went out the door.

"They don't need to know your whole history, Andrew," Emma said when we were in the hallway.

"I didn't want poor Ronnie to continue with the mistaken notion that he was the bad boy in the office," I said with a wry grin.

Emma laughed. "Your desire for confession is admirable, Andrew, but you have already made sufficient restitution for your past misdeeds."

"Okay."

Emma led me down the hallway to the corner office of the psy-unit's director. Nathaniel Parker saw us approaching and came to the office door to greet us.

"Emma, I'm glad to see that you're back from your trip," he said. "And I don't need to use telepathy to tell that this must be our new team member." Nathaniel extended his hand. "Welcome aboard, Andrew."

"Hello, Mr. Parker," I said, shaking hands with him.

"You can just call me 'Nathaniel.' "

"Thanks, Nathaniel."

"Please come into my office and make yourselves comfortable," he said, gesturing toward two chairs in front of his desk.

Nathaniel Parker was a slender man about 40 years old. He wore wire-rimmed glasses, a tweed jacket, and brown loafers. To me, Nathaniel looked like a college professor who should be teaching an art history class or an English literature class at a college. He certainly did not match my image of what the head of an elite counterespionage unit should look like.

"Andrew, I'm sure that you will be a great addition to our team."

"Thanks. I'm looking forward to helping the team."

"In addition to us, we are training several apprentices. Normally, you would serve eight to ten months in training as an apprentice. However, you have so much ability that we are going to place you on a fast track onto our elite team."

"I'll do my best."

"I'm sure that you'll do well," he said graciously.

"Before I met Emma, I had no idea that telepaths were working for the United States government."

"Seven years ago, I became an NSA agent, I would never have expected to one day be leading a team of telepaths," Nathaniel said. "I didn't tell the NSA about my special abilities because I wanted to blend in with the other agents. I didn't want the NSA to think that I was crazy or a freak. Three years ago, though, I decided that I could be of great service to my country by using my telepathic abilities. I told NSA officials about my abilities."

"I'll bet that didn't go over well," I said.

"You're right," Nathaniel said. "I was almost fired. My supervisor thought that I was insane. I was summoned to discuss my situation with three NSA officials. They planned to suspend or fire me. However, during the hearing, I requested permission of the three officials to demonstrate my abilities. One of them consented to allow me to try to mindjack him. About three seconds later, I took control of him. He and I began to speak the same words in unison. Then I had him do a few push-ups and jog around the room."

"That must have freaked out the other two NSA officials," I said.

Nathaniel nodded. "They were sitting there watching with their mouths open and their eyes as wide as could be. When I released the man from the mindjack, he confirmed what had happened. The hearing was adjourned, and I was not suspended. For the next three weeks, nothing happened. Then I was summoned to a meeting with the director of the NSA, the White House security advisor, and other officials. They explained that in recent months there had been many inexplicable, violent incidents in the United States and some other countries. After reviewing the cases, they were convinced that mindjackings had occurred."

"They were probably right," I said.

"Yes, they were. And they were very worried. They felt that the United States was almost defenseless against such attacks. Therefore, because of my abilities, they asked me to create a telepathic unit in the NSA. I was appointed as the head of this special unit."

"Instead of getting fired, you got promoted."

He chuckled. "Yes."

"On our way to see you, Andrew and I stopped for a visit with the apprentice class," Emma said. "Andrew met Julie and all of her students."

"Oh, good," Nathaniel said. "I'm glad that you met them, Andrew. At the present time, Emma, Julie, and I are taking turns teaching the apprentice class. All our other psy-ops agents are out in the field, primarily in defensive positions at the White House, Pentagon, and CIA headquarters. Our resources are stretched very thin. We need to get those apprentices trained as quickly as possible, then get them out in the field."

"In response to the threat posed by terrorist telepaths, we embedded seven psy-ops agents with the Secret Service. We are concerned that the terrorist telepaths might mindjack a Secret Service agent and force that agent to open fire on the President, Vice-President, or some other government leaders."

"That is a very valid concern," I said. "The terrorists are almost certainly going to attempt some assassinations."

"Hopefully, our embedded psy-ops agents will be able to stop any assassination attempts."

I nodded. "I hope that they can. It would be disastrous if the terrorists mindjacked a Secret Service agent."

"We have five psy-ops agents embedded with the CIA," Emma continued. "And we have three agents working at the Pentagon. Both the CIA and the military want more psy-ops agents, so we're going to recruit more apprentices. We are currently training seven apprentices. All of us in this office help with the training. Since we all have different abilities and different backgrounds, it is valuable for the apprentices to receive instruction from different trainers."

"Am I going to train some apprentices?" I asked.

"Eventually," Nathaniel said. "At the moment, though, you are more of a trainee than a trainer. Your telepathic potential is great, but you have much to learn." Noticing my frown, he added, "I have a lot to learn, too. We all have a lot to learn. We are like explorers traveling through an uncharted wilderness."

"We're sort of on a telepathic Lewis and Clark expedition," I said.

"Yes, but we're not searching for the Northwest Passage," Nathaniel said. "We're searching for enemy telepaths. And it's a search-and-destroy mission."

"We have a good team here at the NSA," Emma said. "Hopefully, you'll get to meet the other team members pretty soon."

"All of us have traveled different roads to get

here," Nathaniel said. "Jimmy Dalton is the team leader of our White House unit that is working with the Secret Service. Before coming to work for the NSA, Jimmy was a police detective in Cleveland. He was able to solve cases that no one else could solve. It seemed that he was incredibly intuitive. However, he eventually realized that his powers far exceeded mere intuition."

"The team leader of our Pentagon unit is Ann Jenkins," Emma said. "Before she came to work for the NSA, Ann was a graduate student in the psychology department at Georgetown University. She was doing research into psychic phenomena. Her psychic experiments produced spectacular results. Her results far exceeded the results of the other graduate students. Some persons suspected that she was faking her reports. After conducting more tests, Ann realized that her own telepathic energy was dramatically affecting the results of her research. We found out about her abilities and recruited her to work for us."

"Our class of apprentices shows great promise," Nathaniel said. "I'm optimistic that they will be very helpful when they complete their training. In about a month, Jack, Kristy, and Ronnie will be ready to graduate from apprentice status to full team membership. I might assign all three of them to the CIA because the CIA is in urgent need of our services. Becca, Leslie, and Bryan all have good potential, but they are a bit too timid about using their powers."

"None of those three have been able to mindjack anyone yet," Emma added. "Bryan is excellent at defending himself against being mindjacked, but he needs to learn to be more aggressive."

"And Leslie was making progress before the two recent tragedies," Nathaniel said. "The deaths of Stacey and Rachel are weighing heavily upon her and upon all of us. Apparently, the terrorist telepaths have located our unit. I had hoped that our psy-ops unit would be safe and inconspicuous here. We only occupy one floor in one building on this campus."

"Who are all these other persons that I see on this campus?" I asked.

"We share the campus with a much larger unit whose primary purpose is to defend the United States against biological attacks. About ninety percent of the employees on this campus work for the biohazard defense unit. Since this place has been designed to look like a college campus, we sometimes call them the biology department. We are the psychology department."

"This is a very small, specialized college," I said with a smile.

"Some of our employees joke that since they are at a make-believe college that they will do imaginary work," Nathaniel chuckled. "In actuality, they are dedicated employees who work hard."

"""There is an excellent laboratory here," Emma said. "That laboratory is one of the reasons that we were placed at the same location as the biohazard unit. Our psy-ops unit is hoping to find chemical defenses against telepathic attacks."

"Even if we can't stop a mindjacking by terrorist telepaths, we hope to at least delay the mindjacking," Nathaniel said. "If the person being targeted by the telepaths can resist being mindjacked for a few seconds, then that person will have time to shout out that he is under attack. In addition, if that person is armed, he will have enough time to throw his weapon out of reach before the telepath takes control. This would be especially important for FBI and Secret Service agents."

I nodded. "Yes. Gaining those few seconds could

make a huge difference."

"We are also currently working with scientists at other laboratories to develop a device that detects telepathic energy," Nathaniel said. "These devices could be placed in the White House, Pentagon, Capitol Building, and at the CIA, FBI, and the NSA headquarters at Fort Meade."

"That would be very helpful."

"Eventually we hope to develop a device that generates a dampening field that will block telepaths."

After conversing with Nathaniel for a few more minutes, we said goodbye and left his office. Emma took me to her office, which I would be sharing with her until I got my own office.

Chapter 8

Terrorist Telepaths

After having lunch in the cafeteria, Emma and I walked along a path near the lake. There were several paved paths that could be used for walking or biking. In the lake, there were multicolored Koi fish that could be observed from the ornamental bridge.

"I sometimes bring my bike here and ride along this path," Emma said.

"I occasionally ride my bike in the park next to my condo," I said. "During the warm weather months, I play tennis in that park."

"Living next to that park is like having your own little country club."

"Indeed," I agreed.

"You and I should rent a bicycle-built-for-two and ride it here," Emma suggested.

"You've got to be kidding me."

"I think that it would be fun," she insisted.

"I wonder whether I could mindjack that idea out of your head," I said.

"Go ahead and try. I'll toss you into the lake."

I laughed. "Okay, you win. Let's rent a bicycle-built-for-two."

"Good."

At that moment, off in the distance, I noticed a person behaving oddly on the bridge that spanned a narrow section of the lake.

"That man seems to be having a seizure!" I exclaimed, reaching for my cell phone. "Should we call 911?"

"NSA security will get here a lot faster," Emma said, pulling out her own phone. "And we have a good medical facility on this campus."

While she made the call to NSA security, we ran toward the bridge. As we got closer to the bridge, a look of shock appeared on Emma's face.

"Oh, no!" she exclaimed. "That's Nathaniel!"

"Is he being attacked telepathically?" I asked.

"I'll find out!" Emma squinted as she concentrated on telepathically linking with Nathaniel. After about five seconds, she said, "He is under a telepathic attack! There are at least four telepaths trying to take control of him! They are very strong! I don't know how much longer he can hold out! I'm going to send him some telepathic energy."

"I can help!" I volunteered.

"Yes, please do! The attack has not abated at all. In fact, it seems to have intensified!"

I have never previously formed a three-way telepathic link, but there was no time to ask questions about the process. I telepathically linked with Emma and, as a consequence, found myself also linked to Nathaniel.

Emma and Nathaniel had united their powers to strengthen the shield against the terrorist telepaths. Now that I was part of the mindlink, I felt Emma access my telepathic power and use it to strengthen the shield.

Somehow I could sense that the terrorists were aware that they were now fighting three persons. I perceived their anger and frustration. Suddenly, without preamble, the attack stopped completely.

Emma and I were still about fifty yards from the bridge. Nathaniel staggered against the side of the bridge and leaned on it for support.

I spotted a uniformed NSA security officer hurrying across the bridge toward Nathaniel. I assumed that the man was coming to help Nathaniel. However, the security officer pulled out his pistol and fired a shot at Nathaniel. The shot hit Nathaniel in the right shoulder.

"What is he doing?" Emma cried out. "Stop!"

I was a faster runner than Emma, so I ran ahead onto the bridge. I tried to mindjack the security officer in order to stop him. As soon as I tried, though, I recognized the telepathic presence of the terrorists with whom we had dueled only seconds earlier.

I attempted to wrest control of the security officer's mind away from them. There was no time, though. As the man fired again, I tackled him, knocking off his aim. He didn't completely miss, though.

The second shot hit Nathaniel in the left thigh, causing Nathaniel to fall off the bridge and into the lake.

I slammed two solid punches into the security officer's face. He dropped his gun, and I slapped the gun away. I punched him in the head again, knocking him unconscious.

Emma kicked off her shoes and jumped into the lake. She swam toward the spot where Nathaniel had fallen off the bridge, then she went underwater to rescue him.

In the meantime, I retrieved the pistol that the

security officer had dropped. I wanted to secure the weapon so that it could not be used by anyone else. There were other persons rushing toward the bridge, and any of them could be mindjacked and turned into an attacker.

I walked down to the base of the bridge, then waded into the water in order to help Emma pull Nathaniel out of the lake. When we got him up onto dry land, we applied pressure to the bullet wounds in order to keep him from bleeding to death.

Within a few minutes, an ambulance arrived. The two emergency medical technicians on the ambulance wanted to take Nathaniel to a nearby university hospital.

I expected Emma to object and would want Nathaniel to be taken to the NSA medical facility on this campus. Therefore, I was slightly surprised that Emma allowed Nathaniel to be taken to the university hospital.

At first I reasoned that she had permitted him to go to the university hospital because that hospital would be better equipped than the NSA medical facility. However, as the ambulance pulled away, I deduced her true reason for allowing Nathaniel to be taken away.

“The terrorist telepaths are now targeting the NSA facilities,” I said to Emma. “You believe that Nathaniel will be safer to get completely away from the NSA campus."

She nodded. "Yes. The terrorists apparently have us within their sights. It is alarming that those telepaths were able to locate Nathaniel here on this campus. In fact, it is alarming that they even know who he is. This psy-ops unit is supposed to be top secret."

Emma and I continued our discussion as we went back into the building in order to tell the rest of our psy-ops team what had happened. First, we spoke with Julie Constant and the apprentices. After that brief meeting, Emma used encrypted communication lines to contact our agents who were at the White House, the Pentagon, CIA headquarters, and other locations.

Emma completed these notifications as quickly as possible because she was anxious to get to the hospital. I rode with her there, and we headed directly to the emergency room. We were relieved to learn that Nathaniel was in stable condition and would soon be transferred to the intensive care unit. He was expected to fully recover.

Emma and I went to the visitors' waiting room and sat on a couch.

"At least we now know with certainty that Nathaniel

is not a double agent working for the enemy," I said.

"I knew that with certainty all along," Emma stated firmly.

"At least I now know with certainty that Nathaniel is not a double agent," I amended my comment.

"Right. Now you know."

"The terrorists might stage a phony assassination attempt on their mole agent in order to deflect suspicion from that person. However, that was definitely an authentic attempt to kill Nathaniel." I paused, then added, "We also know with certainty that Nathaniel is a good guy because I probed his thoughts while I was linked to his mind. He is as patriotic as George Washington and Abraham Lincoln."

Emma looked at me. "Hmmm. I'm not sure whether you should have probed our director's mind. However, since you mindlinked with him in order to save his life, I suppose that it was okay."

"While we were mindlinked with Nathaniel, I also was able to scan the thoughts of the terrorist telepaths attacking him," I said. "I can confirm that they do call themselves 'the Jinn.' I was also able to distinguish four individual personalities in this collective entity. They call themselves Effrit, Termagant, Vetala, and Sila. I had the impression that Sila and Termagant were women, but I'm not positive."

Emma's eyes widened in astonishment. "You were able to get all the information while simultaneously defending Nathaniel?"

"I am super cool," I joked.

"Yes, you've mentioned that fact previously. How did you remember all those names?"

"I am super smart."

"Apparently, you are super smart. Unfortunately, you are not super modest."

I laughed. "Maybe not."

"You're dropping this bombshell of information rather casually. Why didn't you mention this an hour ago when we were meeting with the rest of our psy-ops unit?"

"I didn't mention it because the infiltrator is probably in our unit."

Emma frowned. "You made the correct decision by not mentioning it. It now seems likely that we have been infiltrated."

Later in the evening, Emma drove me back to my new apartment.

"This has been quite an eventful first day on the job," I commented wryly. "I hope that tomorrow things are a bit more peaceful."

Emma laughed. "I can assure you that most days at the NSA are more tranquil."

The next day did begin in a calm, ordinary way. Emma picked me up in the morning, and we went to the campus. Most of the morning was spent in conferences about the attack on Nathaniel. We had a video conference with the NSA telepaths working with the Secret Service and the Pentagon. I was glad to meet these other members of our psy-ops team.

Afterwards, as we walked down the hallway, Emma and I saw Becca standing near the room where the apprentice class met. Becca had a dazed, faraway expression as she stared off into space. I was concerned that Becca was being mindjacked, and I was about to spring to her defense.

"Becca, what's wrong?" Emma asked, placing her right hand on Becca's shoulder.

Becca turned her attention toward us, and I could see that she was not under telepathic attack.

"Leslie just called me," Becca explained. "She's in the hospital. Leslie was almost killed!"

"What happened?" I asked.

"While she was driving to work this morning, she felt herself being mindjacked, but she couldn't block it. Someone took control of her and began steering her car. The mindjacker veered the car off the road so that it would go over a cliff!"

"That's terrible!" Emma exclaimed. "How did Leslie survive?"

"The car smashed through the guardrail, but the car got snagged on the torn metal of the guardrail. While it was dangling on the edge of the cliff, some persons pulled Leslie out of her car. Just a few seconds later, the car fell into the ravine and exploded!"

"I'm so glad that those good persons got her out of the car in time," Emma said. "They risked their lives to rescue Leslie."

"I'm so grateful to them," Becca said, managing a smile. "Leslie is my 'Minnesota twin,' so I need her here with me."

Emma hugged Becca. "We need both of our Minnesota twins."

"Thanks."

"Do you want us to drive you to the hospital?" Emma asked.

"No, I'm fine. Leslie is going to be released in about an hour. She just has a few bumps and bruises. I'm going to pick her up at the hospital and drive her home."

We spoke with Becca for a few more minutes, then she left for the hospital. Emma and I decided to go to the cafeteria to discuss the situation. We needed to inform the rest of the psy-ops team about the attack on Leslie; however, since it seemed probable that someone on our team was an infiltrator who had tried to murder Leslie, we needed to be careful about what information we revealed.

Just as we were about to enter the cafeteria, Emma received a call. She glanced at her phone's screen.

"This call is from Tony Caprica," she said. "He's a psy-ops agent working with the CIA in Europe. I'd better bring him up-to-date on what's happening here. Why don't you go ahead and get us a table, Andrew, and I'll join you in a few minutes."

"Okay," I said as Emma answered her phone and walked down the hallway to an alcove where no other employees were nearby.

I entered the cafeteria and purchased a cappuccino.

As I headed toward a table, I felt a spasm go through my body. My left hand jerked sideways, causing me to spill the drink onto the floor. I was startled and embarrassed. I grabbed some napkins and tried to mop up the liquid, but the napkins were inadequate for the task.

"I'll take care of that spill, sir," the cashier said as she approached me.

"I'm sorry."

"Don't worry about it. Spills happen here all the time."

"I'm glad that I'm not the only clumsy oaf."

She laughed as she used a mop to quickly soak up the spilled drink.

After thanking the cashier for cleaning up the spill and for the refill that she insisted upon giving me, I went outside.

I was very concerned about what had just happened. I didn't think that I had any medical problem that would have caused the spasm, but I knew that it was a possibility. However, it had felt like a very brief telepathic incursion against me. I wondered whether the incursion had been designed to probe my defenses before a full-scale attack was launched against me.

My suspicions proved to be well-founded. Perhaps because I had been a criminal for a brief period, I had gained some insight into the criminal mind.

As I reflected upon the situation, I walked along the path near the lake. Some ducks glided along the water, while bees skimmed across the flowers on the shore. The peaceful scene helped me to relax, but the tranquility did not last long.

Before I completed my walk, the Jinn telepaths attacked me with lethal intent. Telepathically-linked terrorists now used all their dark powers to try to destroy me. I perceived with crystal clarity that they were evil. This experience was exactly the opposite of when I shared thoughts with Emma. When she was present in my mind, I sensed goodness, kindness, and brightness of spirit.

Today, here in this place, the truth shone with the brightness of the noonday sun.

Just as had been the case during the attack on Nathaniel, I was also able to distinguish the individual personalities in this collective entity called the Jinn. Effrit, Sila, Termagant, and Vetala were again present. This time, though, they were joined by telepaths called Appolyon,

Ghoul, and Marid.

I called upon all my powers and created a strong shield that initially withstood the combined powers of these seven Jinn. To my surprise, I was successfully holding these evil persons at bay. They were astonished, frustrated, and angry that they could not crush me. Their hatred for me increased steadily as they failed to defeat me.

I decided to take the fight to them. In the preceding days, I had been reluctant to kill the persons whom they had sent to kill me. Today, though, I had no reluctance about making lethal strikes against the Jinn. It would be wrong not to kill them. If they lived, many innocent persons would die.

Their relentless attack was wearing me down, and I knew that I needed soon to break the chain before they broke through my defenses. I scanned the seven and soon found the weakest link. With all my power and with righteous anger, I sent a wave of destructive psychic energy at Vetala.

I felt his mind shatter like a glass hitting a concrete floor. The remaining six Jinn were thrown into confusion and disarray. I wondered whether they were all in the same room or whether each was in a different location.

In either case, for about fifteen seconds, the attack on me abated. During this brief reprieve, I took some deep breaths and prepared for the battle to resume.

My six remaining enemies struck with a precise, powerful attack that almost rendered me unconscious. If that had happened, I would either have been killed or mindjacked by them.

Fortunately, I withstood the attack, then counterstriked. Using most of my remaining energy, I launched an energy wave at Termagant, the weakest of the three who remained. This time, though, they were ready for me. Using their linked powers, they formed a shield that deflected my attack.

I knew that I was in serious trouble. I did not have enough energy to launch another powerful attack, and I doubted that I could withstand too many additional attacks on me. I felt my enemies coalescing power to use against me.

Just a second before they struck, a strong shield slammed into place, protecting me from these enemies. Instantly, I detected the presence of Emma's lovely lifeforce. She was here with me, and she would not allow me to die.

"Andrew, this is Emma. I have linked with you. I can feel your exhaustion. They're going to destroy you if you continue to stand alone against them."

"I know," I wearily told her.

"Give me control."

"All right." I surprised myself by so readily agreeing to relinquish control to her.

I could feel my enemies relentlessly pounding on her shield. If Emma had not intervened, it was likely that I would either be dead or mindjacked by now.

Her strength flowed through me. It was like I had been lost and dying of thirst in the desert, then suddenly come upon a life-giving spring of water.

Our enemies apparently could not detect my mindlink with Emma. I could sense that they were puzzled by my renewed strength. They did not have much time to reflect upon the matter. Soon after her defenses were firmly in place, Emma counterattacked with ferocity.

When they withstood her initial barrage of attacks, I sent her a suggestion.

"Focus upon Termagant. She seems to be the weakest link in the chain."

"Okay," Emma replied.

I felt Emma send a focused beam of telepathic power directly at the woman called Termagant. Emma's power smashed her mind like an eggshell. I didn't know whether the woman had been killed, but I was certain that she would never again threaten us.

As had been the case when they had lost their other comrade, the remaining Jinn telepaths fell into disarray. The attack ended. I waited for it to resume again, but it did not. The remaining five enemies did not want to meet the same fate as the other two. After almost a minute of inactivity, I breathed a deep sigh of relief. It was over, and we had prevailed.

Thanks to Emma, we had won. She was a champion of light and life who could defeat these agents of darkness and death.

Chapter 9
The Rise of the Jinn

During our telepathic battle against the Jinn, Emma had been able to scan some of their thoughts. From the mind of one of the Jinn, Emma obtained an address in Baltimore. Emma arranged with the NSA and FBI to raid this address in hopes of capturing some of the Jinn.

I wanted to accompany Emma on the raid, but she thought that it was more important that I focus on finding the spy who had infiltrated our unit. A heavily-armed team of FBI and NSA agents was going to accompany Emma, so it seemed likely that she would be safe. Therefore, reluctantly I remained behind and applied myself diligently to the task to which I had been assigned.

After doing some online research in our office and reflecting upon the situation, I wandered down the hallway and went into the staff kitchen. Bryan and Becca were seated at the table as they ate lunch.

"Hi Andrew," Becca said. "We heard about what you did yesterday. That was wonderful!"

"Thank you, but Emma deserves most of the credit.

If not for her, things would have gone very badly."

"You're too modest," she said.

"That's the first time anyone has ever said that to me," I grinned. "In any case, I was glad to help destroy those terrorists."

"They deserve to be destroyed, especially after what they did to Stacey and tried to do to Leslie," Becca said.

"Did either of you ever really believe Stacey had died of a cocaine overdose?" I asked.

"Yes, all of us did," Bryan said. "On the day before she died, Stacey had mentioned that she had recently tried cocaine at a party."

"We had no idea that the enemy telepaths were even aware of our existence," Becca said. "In light of recent events, it seems likely that Stacey was mindjacked and forced to overdose on drugs,"

"However, we won't ever know with certainty what really happened," Bryan said. "Perhaps she did use cocaine of her own free will."

"Bryan!" Becca exclaimed. "She did not! Stacey would not."

"She was inexperienced with using drugs, so it would have been easy for her to accidentally overdose.

Right here in this kitchen, she told us about doing cocaine for the first time and that she planned to do it again."

That was the information that I wanted.

"Who was in the kitchen when Stacey said these things?" I asked.

"Bryan and Leslie and I were having lunch with Stacey that day," Becca said.

"Hmmm." I considered that information. "Well, that explains a lot of what happened."

I took him totally by surprise. Bryan almost fell off his chair when he felt the telepathic wave hit him. I tried to mindjack him before he could raise his defenses. Bryan, though, managed to shield me sufficiently that my mindjack was deflected.

He counterattacked with such force that I stumbled backwards, bracing myself against the sink in order to avoid falling. Bryan was a very strong telepath, much too strong to be a mere apprentice. It seemed to me that he was stronger than Emma. I hoped that he was not stronger than I was.

As we engaged in telepathic combat, I recognized his power signature. He was one of the terrorists against whom I had battled the previous day. He was one of the five who had escaped from Emma and me. He was Effrit.

I could feel his anger and his hatred as he attacked with all his strength. If he succeeded in mindjacking me, I knew that he would kill me. I knew his secret.

"What on earth is going on?" Becca exclaimed. "Are you two being attacked?"

"No, we are fighting each other," I told her. "Bryan is a terrorist telepath. He is one of the Jinn. He is the Jinn called Effrit. Bryan mindjacked Stacey and Leslie. When Stacey made those statements about using cocaine, Bryan had control of her. It was he who was speaking. Bryan and the other Jinn retained control of her and, the next day, forced her to purchase cocaine and to take an overdose of cocaine"

"He's lying, Becca!" Bryan lied. "Andrew is the terrorist. After he kills me, he's going to kill you."

Becca looked distraught as she stared at us. She could not decide on which side she should intervene, so she did not telepathically attack either of us or link with either of us.

"Help! Help!" Becca shouted and ran out of the kitchen.

Within seconds after she left the room, I felt Bryan

link with the other Jinn telepaths who had escaped yesterday. I was going to have to duel against the Jinn by myself. I realized that I had made a mistake by attempting to capture Bryan by myself.

As they began their onslaught against me with their combined powers, I decided to change my game strategy. Only one of the Jinn was physically present in the room, and I would deal with him physically.

I rushed forward and slammed my fist into Bryan's nose, breaking his nose. He shouted in pain, and his hands went to his face. My second punch hit him full force in the stomach, and he doubled over and fell against the table, then onto the floor.

His concentration was completely shattered. His telepathic shield disappeared, and Bryan lost his link with the other Jinn telepaths. Before he was able to regain his concentration and reestablish the shield and the link, I mindjacked Bryan. The battle was over, and I had control of him.

Becca came running back into the kitchen. She was now accompanied by the instructor, Julie Constant, and an apprentice, Ronnie.

"Andrew, what is going on here?" Julie asked.

"Bryan was one of the Jinn that Emma and I fought yesterday. He is far stronger than he pretended to be. Along with the other Jinn, he murdered Rachel and Stacey and tried to murder Nathaniel and Leslie."

"Are you certain?" Ronnie asked.

"Yes," I stated. "I have control of his mind. Link with me, and I'll give you access to his thoughts and memories."

"That would be the most efficient way for us to find out about Bryan," Julie said. "Andrew, you can be our guide."

Becca, Julie, and Ronnie linked with my mind, and I led them into Bryan's mind. Within a short while, they realized the truthfulness and accuracy of everything that I had told them. Many of Bryan's thoughts and memories seemed to be locked away in an inaccessible place, but we still gained a lot of useful information.

Due to our telepathic abilities, no doubts remained about Bryan's treachery. He had testified against himself.

After we had explored all his thoughts that were accessible to us, my three companions withdrew from the mindlink. I placed Bryan into a semi-comatose state, then released him from the mindjack.

Julie called NSA security, and three officers took Bryan away.

"How could this have happened?" Ronnie asked.

Julie frowned. "We were infiltrated by our enemies. The NSA is going to need to do more rigorous security checks. Based upon what I could glean from Bryan's thoughts, he mindjacked one of our investigators in order to get through the screening process."

"Yes," Julie said. "Bryan's thoughts have provided us with a goldmine of information. The Jinn thought that they had achieved quite a coup by infiltrating our organization. We will make them regret the day that they decided to send Bryan here. I already have some ideas about how we can use Bryan's information against the Jinn."

After conversing for a few more minutes, Julie and Ronnie went to meet with the rest of our team. Before going to join them in the conference room, I called Emma and told her everything that had happened.

Chapter 10
Transcendence

At about ten o'clock in the evening, Emma arrived at my apartment. I gave her a hug as she came inside.

"How did it go in Baltimore?" I asked as we sat on the couch.

She shrugged. "We got there a bit too late. We went to the address that I obtained from the thoughts of the Jinn. It was a house that several persons rented. The house was empty, and all their stuff was gone. We spoke with the landlord. He said that three men and a woman had rented. The landlord thought that they were graduate students. He gave us their names and the references that they had provided. Of course, the information was almost certainly false. The terrorist telepaths were gone."

"Perhaps before we captured Bryan, he tipped the Jinn off that you were coming," I suggested.

"Yes. That might be what happened. I'm still in shock that Bryan was one of the Jinn. He seemed so meek and mild."

"What is the best way to hide a lion?" I asked.

"I'm too tired to solve riddles, Andrew. I give up. What is the best way to hide a lion?"

"Make him appear to be a lamb."

"I suppose so," Emma said. "Bryan the lamb was actually Effrit the lion. About a half-hour ago, I received a call from the head of the tech team that we sent to Bryan's apartment. The tech team has analyzed Bryan's home computer and found that he visited many radical websites. Last year Bryan was brought into a terrorist group."

"They must have been delighted to find that Bryan was a powerful telepath," I said.

"Yes, undoubtedly," Emma agreed. "And Bryan came to them at the perfect time. Bryan was a useful addition to the Jinn group and fit perfectly into the role of Effrit."

"Will they find a new Effrit or simply eliminate that position?"

She shrugged. "I suppose that we'll have to wait and see. Powerful telepaths are difficult to find. I would suppose that they'll try to replace him if they can."

"The attacks on Nathaniel, Leslie, and me would suggest that Bryan and the other Jinn did plan to kill us off one by one," I said.

"Bryan's betrayal explains how those four hit men knew about you and knew where you lived in St. Louis. Either through reading the mind of someone in our psy-ops unit or by eavesdropping on a conversation, Bryan found out that we had hired you. With good reason, the Jinn feared you because Bryan told them how highly we regarded your potential."

"When I was still in St. Louis, the Jinn couldn't attack me telepathically because Bryan had not met me yet. The Jinn couldn't telepathically find me."

"So they sent the hit team to St. Louis to kill you, but they failed," Emma said. "When you came to our NSA offices here in Maryland, Bryan met you. Then by linking with Bryan, the other Jinn telepaths were able to attack you. You had a telepathic target placed on you by Bryan."

"That traitor placed me directly within the crosshairs of the enemy. He was a tool used by more powerful enemies who remain a threat."

"The Jinn wanted to destroy you because they feared you, but they nevertheless underestimated you."

"I'm awesome." I grinned.

"And as humble as always."

"I'm just kidding. You're the only awesome person in this room, Emma."

"Thank you, Andrew. Actually you're pretty awesome, too, but I want you to be modest about your awesomeness."

I laughed. "Okay."

"You seem to me to be a better man than you were a week ago," Emma said.

"I have become more than I was, but I still feel that I can become more than I am."

"What do you mean?" she asked.

"I had a transcendent experience earlier this evening. About two hours ago, I felt a great fountain of power out there. It seemed so close, yet I couldn't quite reach it."

"What was this fountain of power?"

"I'm not sure. Actually, I was hoping that you could tell me."

"Sorry, I can't help you there. However, it sounds intriguing. This is definitely an area that we will have to explore."

"The power seemed familiar, yet was so far beyond me that it was incomprehensible to me."

"Viva the mysteries," she said.

"Indeed. Mystery after mystery. Adventure after adventure."

"I can't even begin to estimate your potential. You astound me."

"You probably have just as much potential as I do -- perhaps more."

"Thanks," Emma said. "I suppose we'll see. The next time you feel that fountain of power, please link with me."

"I will, of course. It's hard to say when that will happen again. I tried just now and several times earlier today, but I didn't have any luck. When it happened earlier this evening, I was sitting out on my balcony doing a bit of stargazing. Suddenly, I felt the presence of another mind. To tell you the truth, at first I thought that it was you. There was a peacefulness and pleasantness that reminded me of you. However, even though you are powerful, this power was to you like the ocean is to a lovely mountain stream."

"Well, I'm glad that I'm a lovely mountain stream anyway."

"You are the loveliest of mountain streams," I said.

"If I were a trout, you would be the stream to which I would head."

"Thank you, I suppose, for that unusual compliment."

"I'm an unusual guy," I said.

"No one could argue with that statement."

Because we were both tired, Emma kept her visit brief. After we told each other goodnight, she returned to her own apartment a short distance down the road.

The next day on the NSA campus, I spent most of my time doing some research on a computer in the office that I shared with Emma. She was in and out of the office all morning as she carried out varied tasks both on and off campus.

In the early afternoon, after an absence of about an hour, Emma came into the office carrying a couple of bags.

"Did you have any lunch yet, Andrew?"

"No, but I am starting to get a bit hungry."

"Good. Then my timing is perfect. I just went by a deli and bought some gourmet grilled-cheese sandwiches. They are made with brie cheese and fig preserves on raison bread. Nathaniel and Leslie are both back home now, so I'm going to bring bags of sandwiches and lemonade to their apartments." Emma placed a bag on the desktop next to the computer. "I decided to include you in my mission of mercy, so I brought some sandwiches and lemonade for you, too."

"Thanks, Emma" I said, opening the bag and removing its contents.

"You're welcome." She glanced over my shoulder at the computer screen. "What have you been working on so intently all day?"

"I have begun doing some research into telekinesis. It seems to me that we should be able to convert telepathic energy into telekinetic energy."

"Have you been able to move anything with your mind?" she asked.

"Not yet. But eventually I'm determined to push a pencil across the table."

"Good luck."

"I realize that pushing pencils across a tabletop doesn't seem very useful," I said. "However, many great enterprises begin small. Throwing pencils across the room might lead to throwing boulders across a valley."

"Or throwing cars down the street. Or tanks across battlefields. In the near future, the battlefield will be filled with robots, drones, and telepathic warriors."

I nodded. "I can imagine the battles that we would have against enemy telepaths."

"They would be enemy telekinetists," she said.

"Is that a word?"

"Now it is," Emma grinned. "I like to coin words."

"I'll notify the **Oxford English Dictionary** about adding this new word."

"Good," she said.

"When you coin words, you're in good company. Shakespeare, Dr. Seuss, Jane Austen, Lewis Carroll, and J.R.R. Tolkien all invented words. If you call me a 'nerd,' you can thank Dr. Seuss for that word."

"If I call you a 'goofball,' who do I thank for that word?" Emma asked.

"I don't know I'll have to check the **Oxford English Dictionary**."

"Nerd."

"Thank you, Dr. Seuss," I jokingly reminded her.

Emma headed toward the door. "Well, I'd better resume my mission of mercy. I need to deliver this food to

Nathaniel and Leslie. I'm also going to bring them up-to-date on everything that has been happening."

"I'll see you later," I waved to her as she went out the door.

After her departure, I resumed my research and found some interesting articles and videos. At about four o'clock in the afternoon, I felt like I was at a good stopping point and logged off the computer.

I got up and walked out of the office with the intention of going to the cafeteria to purchase a soda. As I started to head down the hallway, though, I saw Emma at the far end of the hallway.

Upon spotting me, Emma waved and began walking toward me. Then, to my horror, a look of consternation appeared on her face, and she collapsed onto the floor. As I ran toward her, I sent my consciousness ahead of me and linked with her mind. I was startled to find that she was under attack by all the remaining Jinn.

Our enemies were now joined by someone whom I had not previously encountered. These Jinn were much stronger than previously, perhaps due to the addition of this new telepath. They were angry and seeking revenge.

Almost immediately I realized that these newly-empowered Jinn could easily kill both Emma and me. The Jinn were so intent upon their attack on her that they did not initially notice me. At that point, I could have pulled out of the mindlink and survived. Emma would not have wanted me to die needlessly.

That option crossed my mind, but I never seriously considered leaving. I would not leave Emma to the mercy of the merciless. Even if I were not falling in love with her, I would not abandon a friend. In fact, I would try to help anyone threatened by the forces of darkness.

If the Jinn were going to kill her, they would have to kill me first. I hurled myself wholeheartedly into the mindlink and deflected the attack away from Emma. The attention of the Jinn turned toward me, and that was where I wanted their attention. Through the mindlink, I felt their hatred and their fury.

Within the collective entity that attacked us, I could still recognize the individual personalities of the Jinn. Marid and Sila were there as were Appolyon and Ghoul. The powerful newcomer to the Jinn called himself 'Iblis.'

The Jinn hit me with everything they had, and it was a devastating onslaught. These enemies of truth, beauty, and goodness had tapped into the dark power that ruled them.

From their mystical mountain, these enemies of humanity unleashed the full force of evil against me. I staggered and almost collapsed. I realized, though, that if I fell now, neither Emma nor I would ever again get up in this mortal world.

I quickly placed a barricade between myself and the Jinn. As I did so, I understood the futility of forming the barricade. I knew that this time my defenses would be inadequate. The Jinn had somehow gained access to too much power. I had built a cardboard hut as a shelter against a hurricane.

As I felt my defenses begin to collapse, I wondered whether there was somewhere that Emma and I could make a strategic retreat. Somehow we needed to find a sanctuary. At that moment, for the second time in my life, I felt the proximity of a great fountain of power.

Like a drowning man grasping for a life preserver, I seized hold of this lifeline and embraced an unknown, mysterious presence. As I did so, I felt the fear and confusion of my enemies. Perhaps they did not understand what I was doing. Or perhaps they understood all too well and that understanding was the source of their fear.

In either case, they had good reason to be afraid. To the extent that I could, I tapped into the power that had arrived so unexpectedly. Before the Jinn could flee, I sent telepathic tidal waves of energy crashing into them. I sought to destroy these servants of evil.

Within seconds, I went from being prey to being the predator, from being the hunted to being the hunter. I annihilated Appolyon and Ghoul, then destroyed Sila. Marid pulled out of the telepathic bond, but I hit him with a backlash of power as he withdrew. I think that he survived, but I felt his telepathic powers implode. It was likely that he had lost his telepathic abilities.

Just as I turned all my attention toward the destruction of the one calling himself 'Iblis,' he vanished like the morning mist. The coward would not stand and fight against someone whom he could not overwhelm. I resolved to deal justice to him some other day.

For now, my main concern was Emma. I focused upon her and sent power into her in order to revive her. She had never completely lost consciousness, and I was always aware of her thoughts as I defeated our enemies.

I cradled her in my arms. To my relief, her eyes opened, and she smiled at me.

"You won," she said.

"We won."

"Oh, yeah. I was a big help flat on my face on the floor."

"The victory today is yours, Emma. I am merely the knight who serves the noble lady."

Emma stood up. "Wow! So that was your fountain of power! Now I understand!"

"Yes, it's certainly an epiphany. How are you feeling?"

"Good."

"Do you want me to drive you home?" I asked.

"No. In a few minutes, we should go tell the rest of the team what happened. They'll be so happy!"

Before meeting with our psy-ops team, Emma and I went outside and sat on a bench near the lake. It was great to spend time with this wonderful woman. My telepathic abilities did not include seeing the future, but I hoped that my future would always include Emma.

She ran her right hand affectionately through my hair.

"Are you ever going to get a haircut?" she asked.

"I've been busy fighting the forces of evil. I haven't

had time to get a haircut."

"Well, you have some time now," she said.

"The two most powerful Jinn got away. I want to get them, too."

"Even if we eventually get them, too, this war will continue."

"Yes, that's true, but there are a limited number of persons with telepathic abilities," I said. "It will take a lot of time for the terrorists to find and train a new group."

"Perhaps they have their own group of apprentices. Those apprentices might be promoted and made into the new elite group."

"Hey! You're going to be kicked out of the Young Optimists' Club," I joked.

She laughed. "I wasn't aware that I was a member. However, I consider myself to be an optimistic person. I know that our side is ultimately going to win. And it's good to be fighting alongside such a handsome man with lovely long hair and an attractive beard."

"That's quite a paradigm shift," I said.

"You have a way of changing my perspective."

"Regardless of what awaits us on the road ahead, I'm looking forward to making the journey with you."

"It will be glorious," she said.

"Indeed." I bent forward to kiss her and was pleased when she leaned forward for the kiss.

****

The author's website is **JoeRogers.homestead.com**

Joseph Rogers has other novels and novellas including:

The Chronicles of Caroline Casey

The Magical Truths of Caroline Casey

The Magical Truths of Phoenix Rising

The Magical Truths of Betwixt and Between

The Magical Truths of the Immortal Maiden

Hallowed Eve, Hallowed Day:

A Supernatural Suspense Story

Realm of Haden: A Space-Age Fantasy

Maiden of Orleans: A Bayou Thriller

The Snow Maiden: A Suspense Thriller

Moonlight Warriors: A Tale of Two Hit Men

The Powers Unseen: A Supernatural Thriller

Made in the USA
Monee, IL
15 October 2024